AUTUMN IN SUNSET HARBOUR

CP WARD

"Autumn in Sunset Harbour"
Copyright © CP Ward 2022

The right of CP Ward to be identified as the Author of this Work has been asserted by him in accordance with the Copyright, Designs and Patents Act 1988.

All rights reserved. No part of this publication may be reproduced, stored in a retrieval system, or transmitted, in any form or by any means without the prior written permission of the Author.

This story is a work of fiction and is a product of the Author's imagination. All resemblances to actual locations or to persons living or dead are entirely coincidental.

AUTUMN IN SUNSET HARBOUR

For Mr. and Mrs. Armitage
the two best (and scariest!) teachers I ever had

And for Dave
miss you, mate

1
COMING HOME

It was the phone call Rachel Castle had been dreading. All too predictably, it came at a time when she was already at a low, having just returned from a morning sitting in the Job Centre. She had been filling out forms for potential employment from the start of October, now that summer was in its death throes—

Oh, don't mention death.

'Rachel, dear, I'm sorry to have to tell you this, but it's about Grandma....'

Bethany, her flatmate, had spotted the sudden lurch in emotion straight away, and was holding out a glass of wine almost before Rachel's mother, Linda, had delivered the bad news. Rachel, one hand on the back of the nearest chair, was trying not to cry.

'I'm afraid she passed away this morning. We were all quite surprised. She was always a healthy old thing, wasn't she?'

Was, was, was. All it would be from now on. Rachel's beloved grandmother, Marigold, at times, when her mother was working two jobs to make ends meet, more like a mother than her own, was gone.

'Was … was ….'—the word wouldn't leave her alone—'Was … it quick?'

'She died in her sleep. Natural causes. The way we all want to go if we have the option of choosing, don't we?'

Rachel wasn't in a question-answering mood, so just muttered, 'Ahh.'

Linda, however, seemed in the mood to ask them. 'So, how was your summer job? I take it you've finished for the season now? Have you found another job yet?'

'Uh, not yet, but I'm in the process of looking—'

'Oh, that's great. So you're free to come down for the funeral next weekend then?'

The summer job at a campsite called Tall Trees Lake Premier had tied her over for a couple of months, but that now she was back in Brentwell, living with Bethany, she needed to start saving her pennies. Bethany had Airbnbed her room over the summer, but she couldn't afford to give any concessions on the rent.

'Ah, the funeral? It's next weekend?'

When train prices would be highest. She could drive, of course, but petrol was through the roof and the road was a nightmare.

'Yes, Saturday afternoon. You could come down Thursday or Friday. Come on, dear, we haven't seen you in ages.'

Rachel winced. The last thing she needed was an expensive trip home, but it was Grandma's funeral. She couldn't miss it.

'Okay,' she said, giving a dizzy nod, aware that her legs could wobble and fall out from under her at any moment. Luckily Bethany had put the glass of wine down and was standing nearby, ready to catch Rachel, just in case.

'Thank you, dear,' Linda said. 'It'll be lovely, you'll see. We'll see her off right.'

She hung up. Rachel stared at the phone in her hand, then turned to Bethany. Before she could say anything, she burst into tears.

∼

'Look at these I found in the little cake shop on the corner,' Bethany said, sliding a tray out of a small cake box. 'Maple and pecan fruitcake. I got us three, one each and one to share.'

'I'm going to miss you,' Rachel said, as Bethany handed her a spoon. 'I'm so sorry I have to go again so soon.'

Bethany shrugged. 'I'll have to Airbnb your room for a bit,' she said. 'I hope you don't mind.'

'Just no more weirdoes,' Rachel said. 'That last one failed to convert me.'

'Oh, you mean the Bird Watcher's Bible he left in your top drawer?' Bethany smiled. 'Alex. He was all right. I mean, I wasn't about to go out with him or anything, but he was a bit different.' She sighed. 'A shame, he said he was moving to Romania. Perhaps he was going to spot some vampire bats. How long do you think you'll be gone?'

'A week, tops. I mean, I like my home village and everything, but there's nothing much there. Mum wants help going through Grandma's things, but that should only take a few days.'

'Sure, just let me know, and I'll kick out whatever touring rock band I've got staying in your room.'

'Thanks.'

'I hope it goes well.'

'Me too.'

'Right, let's eat this cake before it goes warm.'

~

In the end, against her better judgment, but in the hope of saving some money on the train fares that just seemed to get more expensive by the day, she decided to drive. From Brentwell there was no easy road; whoever had designed the transport routes across Devon and Cornwall had perhaps dropped their pen on the map somewhere between Plymouth and Porth Melynos, creating a violent explosion of tiny lines, all of which had materialised into a couple of dozen miles of winding lanes with blind corners and hairpin bends, miles at a time with nowhere to pass, and random hazards such as overgrown ditches invisible until you were plunging into them, and unkempt hedgerows of thorn bushes that could strip the paint clean off any car forced in too close. The train took the luxurious route down to Plymouth and then along the coast, but the way by road was an exercise in patience and nail-biting nerves.

She set off early on Friday morning, driving southwest out of Brentwell, through Willow River, and then down around the eastern edge of Dartmoor. She paused at a pretty café on the edge of the moor to get a coffee and prepare herself for the challenge ahead. Already her phone reception was starting to weaken; by the time she made it home it would be just a memory. Still, it might be better to get off the grid for a bit, although, on the other hand, if she couldn't bury herself in her phone, she might be coerced into talking to people. How many of her old school friends would show up at Grandma's funeral?

The fewer the better, but it would be against her natural run of luck to assume anything.

Finishing her coffee, she took one last look at the final decent view before Porth Melynos, then climbed back into her car and set off. In her little Fiesta she at least had a car of appropriate size for the 'Tangle', as she liked to call it. She had only been driving for five minutes before she found her way blocked by an inappropriately sized people carrier. It took ten minutes of backing up and squeezing into hedges before she was able to let the smiling, waving woman and her seemingly empty monstrosity past. From there she had roughly five minutes of peace before a herd of sheep held her up for another fifteen minutes. An old farmer knocked on her window with the hook of a shepherd's crook and asked if she knew someone called Kate from Holford Secondary, to which she smiled and shook her head.

And then, the jewel in the crown, the shining star at the top of everything: she ran over a nail.

After a couple of minutes of urging her poor, groaning car along the narrow road, she managed to find a farm gateway. She pulled in, climbed out, and went around to the boot to fetch the spare tyre.

By the time she was finally done—one sore and broken nail and one bruised knee from dropping the spare later— she was tired, frustrated, getting hungry, and the sun was low in the sky. The only thing worse than driving the Tangle by day was driving the Tangle by night, with the sizes of her opponent cars impossible to see behind their glaring, always-full-beam lights, and the additional threat of animals or even pedestrians appearing out of nowhere.

She climbed back in, wiped sweat off her brow, took a deep breath, and started the engine.

It started. All good. She pulled out from the gateway just as two cyclists on racing bikes came haring around the corner, narrowly missing her. The second turned and shouted something unpleasant, but was out of sight around the next bend before Rachel could think of a suitable reply.

The sun dipped into the tops of the hedgerows as she set off again, frequently blinding her as it glittered through the thorn bushes. She thought about just giving up for the night, pulling in somewhere and sleeping awkwardly in the car, but she really wanted to get there tonight, so she gritted her teeth, willing herself forward, and a couple of minutes later the road finally opened out. A valley dropped away in front of her; nestled into its hollow was her home village, a cluster of houses and shops on the South West Coast Path tourist circuit, all centered around a tiny harbour with its jutting concrete breakwater and towering cliffs on either side.

As she turned a corner to the top of the road snaking down the valley side into the village, she saw the familiar sign:

Porth Melynos
Welcome to Sunset Harbour

It wasn't a direct translation. In old Cornish, Porth Melynos roughly translated to Port Yellow Night, but some long-ago village council had decided that wouldn't attract enough tourists. Sunset Harbour it had become, despite the fact that for most of the year the sun actually set over the western cliffs rather than over the narrow sliver of sea, a tiny piece of Americana in a place that was very, very British.

She couldn't help but smile. Despite having moved away at the earliest opportunity, it always felt nice to be back.

It was home, after all.

2

A FUNERAL AND OTHER DISASTERS

THAT THE CREMATORIUM WAS FULL ONLY MADE RACHEL feel worse. Grandma Marigold had made a lot of friends over her eighty-seven years it seemed, and they had all brought their extended families to see her off on her final fiery journey. Seeing the chairs full of mourners somehow made Rachel feel like Grandma no longer belonged to her, that in the years since she had moved out of the village the love and joy that Grandma had brought into her life had become available by open invitation. Now, heartbroken, she watched as every man and his dog, and even his dog's fleas got up to say a few words.

Mr. Harding, the greengrocer: 'She was never without a smile. Every morning we'd go through the same routine. "How's the weather looking today, Marigold?" "Well, it must be sunny judging by your smile." She was a delightful woman, and I'll miss our chats over a bag of carrots.'

Mike, who'd delivered the newspaper: 'She never failed to leave me a pound tip at Christmas, Easter, and all the bank holidays. And there'd be a birthday card standing on top of the post box once a year. I don't know how she knew, because I never told her. I guess she must have done a background check.'

Mr. Wilmot, who ran the local chip shop: 'I hadn't seen her in a while—it was a cholesterol thing, I believe—but I remember once in around 1994 she stopped by and bought a small portion plus some mushy peas, and told me they were the best fish'n'chips west of Plymouth Sound, which was a *sound* I liked to hear....'

And so it went on. A local farmer stood up and described how he'd once shared a pleasant good morning with Grandma as she cycled past his tractor, circa 1986. A local fisherman recalled how he'd seen someone from his boat whom he *believed* had been Grandma, fishing off Silly Point, the last reachable section of rock out on the cliffs beyond the breakwater. She'd smiled or waved or something. And a local delivery driver recounted in unnecessary detail how he'd definitely driven past her a couple of times, and how she'd looked like such a wonderful person even though they'd never spoken, or indeed even made eye contact.

Such was the effect Grandma had had on people.

And finally, mere moments before Rachel was planning to jump up and ask the funeral director to make a little room in Grandma's coffin, the curtain was pulled across, and the old dear was sent on her way.

'Are we going to the pub now?' Rachel asked her mother, who was sobbing into a tissue.

'All you young people do is drink,' Linda sniffed.

'All you old people do is talk,' Rachel replied, then felt a pang of guilt as Linda burst into more tears.

~

An hour later, after the cremation was completed, Rachel

and Linda made their way down the hill from the church to the Horse and Buoy Inn, a beautiful old pub in a stonewalled building by the harbourside, for Grandma's wake. Even more people had shown up, spilling out into the beer garden to the pub's side and rear, enjoying a warm September afternoon. As she looked along the harbourside at the patch of shingle beach and the handful of fishing boats moored up against the breakwater, the towering cliffs that made a natural harbour, and the narrow sliver of horizon between them, part of her felt happy to be back. After university had ended she had stayed away, failing to do anything with her degree in Contemporary Journalism, taking temp job after temp job in the hope that something rewarding would come along. Her last short-term contract had abruptly ended in May, but rather than come running home to Porth Melynos, she had found a summer job on the edge of Bodmin Moor. Three months of waiting tables for extremely rich and obnoxious people later and she was unemployed again. The discussion with her mother was coming for sure, but Rachel hoped it would at least hold off until after Grandma's ashes had been scattered.

'Rachel? Is that you?'

The familiar voice sent a shiver running down the back of Rachel's spine, all the way to her knees, which threatened to buckle, throwing her face forwards onto the flagstones. *No, it can't be. Not now. Not here.*

She turned, and there he was. Gavin Benson, the man who had stolen her heart at sixteen and never really given it back. He was taller than she remembered, more angular around the jaw, wider at the shoulders, but the eyes, the smile, the cheekbones, even the curl of hair she had once liked to play with, they were all still there. Inwardly, Rachel swooned. If perfection could have been improved upon, it clearly had been. Gavin was such a dish she could have covered him in ketchup and eaten him in one single bite.

'Gavin? You've—'

'Grown up?' He smiled, and inside Rachel died. 'Yeah, I suppose. I'm working on Dad's boat now.' He clenched a fist. 'Hauling those ropes puts the meat on. I've told him to buy a motorised pulley but he said I'd end up like old George.'

It was nailed home to Rachel how long she'd been away in that she had no idea what he was talking about.

'Wow, that's great,' she said, trying not to eye him up and down, aware that Grandma had been a playful old thing and probably would approve if Rachel tried to sneak Gavin back to hers for a bit of entertainment while her mother was out. 'And you look great. Really great.'

'You do too. You're ... glowing. Did you quit drinking?'

Rachel held off a frown and instead gave Gavin an ambitious smile. 'Yeah, well, I don't have much time for it now, with work and all that.'

The truth—that her salary over the summer had been so low that alcohol had become a luxury item—wasn't something she was about to share.

'Oh?' Gavin said. 'What is it you do now? Did you get that literary critic job at *The Guardian*? I bumped into your mum the other day and she told me it was only a matter of time.'

'Ah, not yet. I'm ... ah ... currently between jobs.'

'That's too bad. Perhaps you could come home for a while. I know Geoff in the pub was looking for someone for a few hours a week. Wouldn't that be great? It would be just like old times.'

Rachel felt a little queasy inside. If he was referring to the same old times she was thinking of, it had been warm summer nights after the pub had closed, down on the patch of shingle below the harbour wall, or the breakwater, or even on the deck of a couple of the fishing boats. Good times. Wonderful times. Hot—

'Daddy!'

'Ah, there's my boy.'

Gavin chuckled as he turned around, scooping a little boy, no older than three or four, up into his arms. Rachel, while internally dealing with a raging storm that was systematically tearing down all her dreams and hopes, could only admit that the lad was a spitting image of his father, apart from the darker hair, which perhaps came from his mother—

'Rachel Castle? Well, I'll be dumped upside down off the breakwater edge.'

No. Please no. Not her. Anyone but her.

The woman was clapping her hands together as she approached. There didn't appear to be a ring on her finger, but it could easily have been buried among the excess flesh of her fingers. Her thick elephantine thighs shuddered, and the curtain of brown hair that fell almost to her waist whipped around her in the only gust of wind along the whole harbour's edge, as though it was trying to blow her off, into the river, down though the seaweed covered rocks, out into the harbour, past the cliffs, and to the open sea, where, joyfully, it would sink her.

Cathy Ubbers smiled and spread her meaty arms wide, as though there was nothing Rachel might desire more in the world than to leap into the embrace of the girl who had tormented her from the first day of secondary school until Cathy had mercifully left school the year Rachel entered the Lower Sixth. Two years older than her, if Rachel had had to wait until the end of time to bump into Cathy again, it would still have been too soon.

But not only was she right here in front of her, in all of

her much-larger-than-life sweaty glory, but she had also swept Rachel's teenage dreams up into a basket, and like Krampus, carried them away for eternal torture.

'Cathy … nice to see you again.'

'Oh, you've met Gavin.' As though Rachel needed to re-meet the man she had been an item with for the last three years of school. 'And this is our lad, Thomas.' With a grin, Cathy patted a stomach that could have hidden a small car. 'Number two is due next month. Are you playing happy families yet?' Cathy gave Rachel's midriff a pointed glance. 'I mean, it looks like it, but they've put out a decent spread, haven't they?'

Rachel winced. 'Only with the one in my head.' Then, clapping her hands together in an embarrassing parody, she added, 'Well, it was lovely to see you guys again, but I'd better go and mingle.'

And get as drunk as is morally possible at my grandmother's funeral.

'Sure,' Cathy said, as though they had once been best friends. 'See you in a bit, yeah? We have so much to talk about. All that catching up to do. Gosh, has it really been six years?'

Six glorious, torment-free years. Rachel spread her hands. 'Where does the time go?'

Cathy glanced at Gavin and winked. 'Well, I know where a fair bit of ours goes, if you know what I mean.'

Unsure what kind of expression was appropriate in response, Rachel glanced at little Thomas, who'd wisely wandered off in the direction of a couple of loitering seagulls.

'Right, mingle,' she muttered, then turned away before the urge to throw herself off the harbourside became too great to resist. It was only a metre and a half to the water, but perhaps if she took a running jump and attempted to land on her head—

'Oh, Barbara, there you are,' Cathy gasped with stage-worthy dramatics' at an older woman wandering down the harbourside. 'Isn't it so terrible? But so lovely that we're all united in our grief.'

While Cathy went to embrace this unfortunate newcomer, and Gavin was distracted rescuing Thomas, whose ice lolly had become a seagull target, Rachel took her chance to escape.

∼

'I'll have a pint, please, Simon.'

The man behind the bar scratched at a wispy beard that was wholly inappropriate on a face that was no more than eighteen years old.

'Ah, do you have I.D.?'

'Simon, it's me, Rachel Castle. You know who I am. I was five years above you in school. I once took you to the school nurse after you got stung by a wasp in the playground.'

'Yeah, but you still look pretty young. And it's the rule.'

'Come on, Simon. I need that pint.'

'Just show me some I.D.'

'I left my purse at home. This is my grandmother's wake. If you look me up on Facebook you can see a picture of my university degree.'

'I'm not allowed to check my phone at work. But even if I could, you can't get reception down here.'

Rachel sighed. 'Nothing's changed then? Except you can't get served in the pub?'

'I'm sorry. Don't you have a driver's license or something?'

'Yeah, in my purse.'

'You could go back and get it, couldn't you?'

'I'd rather jump under a tractor.'

They appeared to have reached a stalemate. Simon gave her a resigned shrug. 'You know, I just thought of something. This is technically a private function, which means that children are allowed to drink if a legal adult buys the drink for them, and it's with a meal. And there's a buffet over there—'

Rachel let out an exasperated sigh. 'I am a legal adult, Simon.'

'It was just a suggestion.'

Rachel stared forlornly off into space as Simon went off to serve some other customers. Through a connecting door into a family room, the bereaved guests at Grandma Marigold's wake appeared to be having far more fun than Rachel thought was necessary. She had hoped to have a quiet drink in the regular bar, but it looked like she had no choice but to rejoin the melee.

Her mother was sitting in a corner, talking to a pair of elderly ladies, whom from snippets of overheard conversation Rachel guessed were members of Grandma's old bridge club. Standing behind them, she waved her hand to get Linda's attention.

'Ah, there you are,' her mother said. 'Come and meet Gladys and Silvia.'

'Hello,' Rachel said, forcing a smile for the two old ladies. Then, turning to Linda, she hissed, 'Mum, I have an emergency.'

'Really? What is it?' Linda climbed out of the booth seat and came over. 'Is everything all right? Are you feeling sick? I know today must have been really hard on you—'

Rachel put up a hand. 'It's much worse than that. Mum, I really, really need you to buy me a pint.'

3

OLD SCHOOL NIGHTMARES

DESPITE FEELING A NEED TO ESCAPE FOR AS LONG AS SHE could remember, Rachel had to admit that Sunset Harbour was a beautiful place, and that in autumn it really came alive. Summer was pleasant, but the town was crowded with tourists, and without a proper beach it meant the harbourside and the breakwater were a crush of people eating ice-cream and fish'n'chips while being bombarded by seagulls. On the other hand, winter could be brutal with the raging sea turning the natural harbour into a maelstrom of churning water, those boats that couldn't be pulled up on to the shingle protected only by the concrete breakwater wall. Spring was chilly, the sun slowly appearing above the southern cliffs, but in autumn, the cliffs became a natural bowl to concentrate the sun's heat, making it t-shirt weather sometimes deep into October. And when the leaves began to change, the cliffs and the valley with its deciduous forest, came alive with red, orange and yellow.

After the tourists had gone home, there was no better place to be than sitting on the harbourside wall, watching the fishing boats going in and out, while huge, dapple-coloured cliffs loomed over you.

At least in theory.

Many of the houses were empty out of season these days, sold as holiday homes, and aside from a few who had gone into family-run fishing, tourism, or retail businesses, most young people from Rachel's generation had moved away in search of work.

Sitting with her feet dangling over the harbour wall as she had done countless times as a teenager, the only difference being that the can of beer of old had now been replaced by a paper cup of coffee from a teahouse a little way up the road, Rachel found herself pining for the old days.

Since leaving for university she had always come back a few times a year, but the eternal days of her youth had accelerated quickly with the infrequency of her visits. Grandma, who had once seemed ageless and immortal, had visibly aged with each visit, Redbean, her family dog, had died seemingly abruptly, having jumped from a sprightly ten to an elderly fourteen in what to Rachel had felt like a couple of months, and her mother, once a gung-ho working woman with never less than two jobs on the go at any one time, was now semi-retired, working just three afternoons a week in the kitchens of a local hotel. The carefree life she had grown up with was gone, and a catapult of uncertainties was flinging her ungainly into the future.

Perhaps if she just sat here a while longer, closed her eyes and concentrated, everything would reset to its factory settings, and the best days of her life could begin over again.

'Excuse me, are you Rachel Castle?'

She opened her eyes. A man stood a short way past her,

holding back a poodle that was investigating the harbour wall edge, as if determined to accidentally slip over.

'Sorry, do I know you?'

'It's Francis. Do you remember? Francis Jenkins.'

Rachel stared. 'F … Francis?' she stammered, the cruelty of an old nickname stopped in its tracks. 'Oh, yeah, I remember you. You've … ah … changed.'

With his spectacles, over-round face and slumped shoulders, Francis Jenkins still wasn't attractive, but the kid from her class everyone had called Floppy Frank had most certainly lost a lot of weight.

Francis smiled. 'You can say it, it's fine. I have a t-shirt with it written on that I wear when I run. It motivates me.'

'When you … run?'

Not jog. *Run*. She remembered Floppy's mum had always driven him up the hill to their primary school, otherwise he'd be so sweaty he'd need to change his clothes before class started. Secondary school and the school bus had been a godsend, but not for his waistline. By the fourth year, anyone forced to sit next to him due to an absence of other seats had needed to position themselves with their feet in the aisle, otherwise they would have been at risk of 'touching load', as the other kids put it. Now, Francis could have sat easily in the middle of two seats without touching the occupants of either.

'You run?' Rachel said.

Francis shrugged. 'Not proper races. Not often, anyway. Mostly trail running. The coastal path, moorlands, places like that. I like the views, and it's the hills that really sort you. Do you run?'

Rachel smiled. 'Only for a bus. But I love a good hill,' she said. 'Particularly when viewed from a window.'

Francis laughed. 'Well, you have a lovely day.'

He wandered off down the harbourside, the dog

nosing in the weeds. Rachel watched him go, wondering who else might appear from the woodwork to prove that it was only she who had failed to get anywhere in life. Cathy Ubbers was producing children with Gavin, and Floppy Frank was now Fitness Francis.

A bright sun was sitting high in the sky. Rachel took a deep breath, relishing both the freshness of the air and the salty smell of the sea. Life could be worse, she supposed. As she climbed to her feet, she wondered if she ought to begin the leaf turning over process by hiking up the coast path to one of the headlands, then smiled and shook her head. In order to change her life, she would need to find the internal motivation to do it over and over, just once wasn't enough.

She walked up into the village and went into the Sunset Harbour Coffee and Fudge Company, a little café and confectionary shop on the corner where the road turned sharply and crossed over a bridge. Coffee and fudge for breakfast was definitely a good idea. It might shock her into changing her life, and well, if it didn't, at least it would cheer her up.

'Rachel Castle? Is that you?'

Rachel stared in disbelief at the old woman standing behind the counter. Gone were the spectacles that used to hang low over a pointed nose. Gone were the ruler-straight curtains of black hair that had once hidden the woman's face, now replaced by a neat, greying bob. Gone even was the witch-like wart that had once protruded from her cheek. In its place was a light dusting of rouge, turning what had once been a fearsome monstrosity into something rather more aesthetic.

For Rachel, though, the memories ran deep. Her hands shook and she took a step backwards towards the door, even as the old lady clapped her hands together and began to laugh.

'Oh dear, so you remember me?'

'Uh….'

'Mrs. Simcock,' the woman said. 'Although these days Valerie is perfectly acceptable.' The woman leaned forward, tilting her head, and Rachel trembled with fear. She remembered that glare from her Year One science class, although what had once been a soul-withering glower capable of drawing all life and vitality out of its targets, had softened a little with age. Now Rachel felt merely scared.

'Mrs….'

'Best to stick with Valerie,' she said. 'It'll be easier for the PTSD.'

'Val—'

'Valerie, not Val. What would you like, dear?'

'To be released from your spell?' Rachel muttered, taking a tentative step forward, in the direction of a counter that groaned under the weight of freshly prepared fudge, the intoxicating aroma of which was making her dizzy.

'What's that, dear?'

'Ah, a latte, please. And a chunk of original.'

'Would you like to sit inside or out?'

Sitting in would probably be a trigger for the lunchtime detentions she had suffered at Mrs. Simcock's hands, usually for 'failing to reach your potential'—which meant scoring less in a test than Mrs. Simcock felt you were worthy of—but it had just started to spot with rain.

'Over there,' Rachel said, glancing over her shoulder. 'In the corner.'

'The farthest one from the counter?'

'Ah, yes.'

'Certainly, dear.'

She told Rachel the price and Rachel handed over coins in a numb, semi-shocked state, then she was retreating as far from her old school teacher as she could. Mrs. Simcock, once the most fearsome motivation to achieve excellent test scores but now turned coffee shop lady, appeared to be enjoying the experience.

A couple of minutes later, when she came over with a tray, Rachel started having flashbacks to her school days, so much so that when Rachel heard a voice say, 'Would someone like to explain why you and Kevin have almost identical answers?', she could swear the words had been spoken out loud. Only when Mrs. Simcock gave a wide smile and began to laugh, did Rachel realise that they had.

She was still searching for a reply when a curtain opened behind the counter and another old woman appeared. In sharp contrast to Mrs. Simcock, this woman had shimmery golden hair, kind eyes and an even kinder smile. Had the two women been auditioning for roles in a seniors' version of *Wicked*, it wouldn't have taken much to decide which witch was which.

'Valerie, are you tormenting our young customer? You know, we should put a warning note on the sign.'

Mrs. Simcock chuckled. 'Oh, Clara, I was just having a laugh. This one was one of mine, back in the good old days.'

'Rachel Castle,' Rachel croaked. 'I got ninety-eight percent on my science mock exam in Year Five.'

Mrs. Simcock gave a sage nod, then narrowed her eyes at Rachel, her eyelids not closing quite enough, making her resemble a lazy, demonic frog. 'And we had a word about that missing two percent, didn't we?'

Rachel attempted to nod, but her body had stiffened and it came out as more of a shudder.

'Is that so?' Clara rolled her eyes. 'Valerie, you're such a brute.'

'But the employment pool is much better for it.'

Mrs. Simcock finally put Rachel's latte and fudge down on the table and retreated to a more agreeable distance as Clara came out from behind the counter. Rachel felt happier in her presence, as though this second woman was a fairy godmother sent to put up a picket line in the way of the wicked witch.

'I apologise for my sister,' Clara said, confirming Rachel's suspicions that she had stepped out of Sunset Harbour and into a 1940s twilight zone. 'Unlike myself, she never really left the classroom.'

'I was born to rule,' Mrs. Simcock muttered with a sinister smile, then, to Rachel's relief, went back behind the counter and through the curtain, where hopefully she would be caught, trapped, and then eaten by a giant spider.

'Were you a teacher too?' Rachel asked.

'Yes, Brentwell Primary,' Clara said. 'I actually only just retired this past July.' She chuckled. 'I can only imagine how my replacement is getting on with those toerags I used to teach. You know how it is, though, it's hard to just stop after a lifetime of work. Valerie and I bought this little teashop last year, and figured it would give us something to do in retirement. We didn't realise how busy this village would be during the summer, though. It was chaos.'

Rachel nodded. 'Autumn is the best season by far. It's still warm, but there are none of the crowds.'

'Are you a local? I haven't seen you in here before.'

'I was. I grew up here. Actually, I live in Brentwell now.'

'Oh really?'

'Just off Porter Street.'

Clara chuckled. 'Oh, where they have that hideous portacabin they call a community centre?'

Rachel smiled. 'That's the one.'

'It's not a bad town otherwise. I was happy there for a long time. I'll be visiting again in a few weeks for my old school's harvest festival, but otherwise, I don't miss the hustle and bustle.'

'It's not exactly London.'

'It is compared to this place. Well, outside the summer months. Did you move back down?'

Rachel shook her head. 'My grandmother passed away. I'm just down for her funeral. I'm going to help my mother for a few days clearing out the house, but then I'm going back up to Brentwell.'

'Oh, that's a shame. I'm very sorry to hear that. What is it you do up there in Brentwell?'

Rachel grimaced. 'Actually, I'm between jobs right now.'

'Really? What a terrible world it is we live in. Well, just give me a shout if you want a bit of extra money. We could find you a few hours here in the Fudge Company, I'm sure. We're not in this to work too hard. It's a hobby really. And I'm sure a pretty face like yours would attract a lot more customers than us two old bags.'

Rachel went bright red as Clara gave a lighthearted chuckle. 'I'm really not planning to stick around long—'

'You must have a boyfriend. I didn't notice a ring on your finger. What's he playing at? Kick him out, I say. Find someone more deserving.'

'It's not like that—'

'Or set fire to his car and kidnap his cat,' Valerie said, reappearing through the curtain, having perhaps managed to kill the giant spider with a violent stare and then shaken off the remaining cobwebs. 'That'll teach him.'

'I don't have a boyfriend right now.'

'There must be someone. There are plenty of eligible young men around here. What about young Francis?'

'She was talking to him outside,' Valerie said. 'I saw it in my crystal ball.'

'Francis is a nice lad,' Clara said.

Rachel was just about to reply when the door opened and Cathy Ubbers marched in, crossing the floor in three huge, inflated strides, one hand coming to rest on the glass countertop a little more heavily than was necessary.

'Morning, Clar, Val,' Cathy said. 'I need three coffees for the launderette on the double. Two black, one white. Oh, and give us a bag of crumbly.'

'Good morning, Catherine,' Clara said a little too sternly, as Valerie, scowling but moving like a reluctant but well-trained dog, went back behind the counter to fulfill the order. 'How are you and the little ones today?'

Cathy gave an overpowering guffaw as though it was the funniest joke in the world. 'The one on the outside had a tantrum before school. The one on the inside is being a lot better behaved, even if I did chunder my breakfast into a bucket behind the dryers half an hour ago.' She started laughing again, then added, 'It had only been in there ten minutes. If I'd had some milk handy I might have gone for another go.'

'Small mercies for the decline in milk rounds,' Clara said, turning away slightly and giving Rachel a sly wink.

'It's a good think Gav's such a love. Honestly. He whisked Thomas off to nursery, came back and gave me a shoulder rub. *Oh.*'

Cathy had turned enough to finally catch sight of Rachel sitting in the corner, trying to hide behind her slice of fudge, but failing when it abruptly snapped in half and came crashing down on her plate with a loud clink.

Reaching up, Cathy theatrically cupped her face with her palms. 'Rach, sorry, I didn't see you there.' She turned to Valerie, who was standing behind the counter, and said in a loud whisper, 'They used to be an item.' Then, raising her voice as though it could mask anything previously said, she added, 'Just those coffees, then!'

'And the fudge?' Valerie asked.

'Of course.'

'Just a moment, please.'

'I don't want to upset her,' Cathy scream-whispered again as Valerie set to making the coffees from a machine behind the counter.

'Always lovely to see you, Catherine,' Clara said. 'How's business?'

'Booming,' Cathy said. 'Autumn, innit? Nothing'll dry and the muck spreaders are out, getting ready for a bit of winter planting. Although, to be honest, I think most people just come in for the conversation.'

'I don't doubt that.'

'I think people see me as a kind of hub for what's going on around here. I mean, it's good to be in the know, isn't it?'

'Quite, quite.'

'So, what's news with you two?'

Clara just shook her head. 'You know retirement, dear. Nothing much goes on.'

'Here you are,' Valerie said, not a moment too soon for Rachel's liking. 'Three coffees, and a bag of crumbly.'

'Nice one, Val,' Cathy said, taking the paper bag and turning to face Rachel. 'Rach, stop by for a natter if you've not got anything on. I heard you were single. We'll see if we can sort you out. You remember Benny?'

'Goodman?'

'Yeah, Benny Goodman. He's still single, innit?'

'Didn't he lose two fingers in a threshing machine?'

Cathy rolled her eyes. 'He lost his fingers, not his—'

Valerie clapped her hands together sharply as though shooing off crows. 'Goodness me, Clara! We forgot to order the clotted cream. I'll get the phone. Cathy, dear, we've loved talking to you, but we've got to get this order in or there'll be a lot of unhappy hikers come Monday morning.'

'Better be getting back anyhow,' Cathy said. 'Those sheets won't dry themselves. Rach. Don't forget about that natter.'

Rachel forced a smile. 'I won't.'

Order in hand, Cathy hustled and bustled her way out of the shop. Clara turned to Rachel. 'I think I'll turn the closed sign round for half an hour or so,' she said. 'A bit of peace and quiet would be nice, wouldn't it?'

Rachel smiled. 'Thanks.'

4

UNCOVERED MEMORIES

GRANDMA MARIGOLD HADN'T QUITE LIVED IN AN ACTUAL castle, but had her erstwhile house contained arrow slits and been topped with battlements, it wouldn't have fallen far short. Set into the hillside halfway up the valley, it hung precariously out over a steep, wooded slope, seemingly forever only a nudge away from capitulation. From the road down into the village it appeared to be a single-storey bungalow, but from the hill's angle it was two, almost three. The lower storey was little more than a cellar and storeroom, however, with Grandma having lived on the upper floor that stood level with the road.

Encircling the outer side of the house, was a garden steep enough to make sieging armies weep. Steps had been cut into the ground at the top and bottom ends, with the rest being a patchwork of terraced flowerbeds and vegetable gardens, with patches of steep lawn or assorted shrubbery thrown in. As a child Rachel had loved it; while it had been useless for any kind of chasing game, they had played a variety of forty-forty, with the home base being the drainpipe on the outer corner by the front gate. Races up the hill had been common between those on catching duty and those hiding behind the shrubs halfway down.

Now, though, the garden that Grandma had tended with such pride looked overgrown and neglected. As they came in from the road and stood at the top of the steps leading down, Rachel's mother put a hand on her lower back and winced.

'I don't know how she managed it,' Linda said. 'Just the thought of walking up and down that garden every day gives me cramps.'

Rachel smiled. 'Well, she was so old that I suppose the river valley hollowed itself out around her,' she said.

'I certainly don't remember it being so far down to the harbour when I was a girl,' Linda said. 'I used to ride my bike up that hill. Now I struggle to make it in the car.'

'You're not going to sell this place, are you?'

Rachel had never thought about it before, but now that she stood on Grandma's doorstep, the thought of losing such an integral part of her childhood filled her with dread.

Linda shrugged. 'I don't know, dear. It's still early days, isn't it?'

'You could live here yourself, Mum.'

Linda shook her head. 'I don't think so. I mean, I grew up in this house, but going back again….' She shook her head. 'Too many memories. Not to mention that I probably couldn't afford it. She used to tell me that the Council Tax was like having a dragon living downstairs, eating up half of her pension.'

Rachel nodded as Linda turned and let herself in. They didn't talk about the circumstances surrounding her mother's flat on the other side of the valley. Linda, fiercely independent, had always been happy there, and that was it. It had been enough for the two of them while Rachel was growing up, but they'd spent many an evening at Grandma's, sitting at the living room table with the lights of the village glittering in the valley below. If Rachel were honest about it, many of her best childhood memories originated there, but, particularly where Linda was concerned, honesty was overrated.

'How long do you think it'll take to go through Grandma's things?' Rachel asked, as they went down the narrow hall and into the cluttered living room with its panoramic bay windows. They were so high up the valley on the eastern side that the sea was visible above the lower cliffs to the west. Grandma had claimed on a clear day you could see as far as France, even though Rachel had stopped believing it once she had started learning geography at primary school.

Linda shrugged. 'She wasn't much of a hoarder,' she said. 'I mean, it looks like there's a lot of stuff here, but it's all kind of condensed into a couple of rooms and the cellar. I imagine we'll be through it all by the end of the week.'

'That's good,' Rachel said, a little more eagerly than she meant. 'I was hoping to get back up to Brentwell by Thursday. I … ah … have an interview on Friday.'

'Really? That's great. What's that for, the Bristol Evening Post? I always knew you'd end up working for a famous newspaper.'

Rachel became a fence post, battered down by a mallet of expectation. She would have gladly taken her mother's idea of famous over the reality: It was as a button pusher for an insurance company, set up by her temping agency, a job so bland she couldn't even remember the company's name.

'Not much point talking about it unless I get it,' she said.

'I suppose not. Well, shall we have a coffee and then get started? Mum lifted a bag. I picked up a couple of walnut Danishes from the bakery. We can't really get to work on an empty stomach, can we?'

Rachel, who could still remember the taste of the fudge less than an hour before, shrugged. 'We've got to keep our strength up, haven't we?'

∽

Grandma Marigold, it turned out, had been more of a hoarder than either of them had realised. Luckily, she had been extremely organised, and boxes of old jam jars, gifted tea towels and unwanted trinkets were so neat they could be carried straight from the cellar to the nearest charity shop. As they delved deeper, however, uncovering items from Rachel's childhood, the nostalgia began to deepen.

'I remember this bear,' Rachel said, holding up a battered teddy bear, faded on one side by the sun. 'Whenever I stayed at Grandma's, she'd let me take him in the bed. Otherwise he always sat in the window, facing south.'

Linda put down the duster she was holding and smiled. 'Michael. That was his name. She said he was waiting for his love to come back from overseas.'

'Was he yours as a child?'

Linda chuckled and shook her head. 'No. I was there when we found him, though. I can't have been more than five. When would that have been? I suppose in the late sixties. We were in a café … I forget where. Plymouth, maybe? There was a little girl in a pram on the table next to us, and she had two bears, a pink one and a blue one. As they were going out of the door, the girl must have dropped the blue one on the floor. I remember Mum picked it up as we were leaving and looked for the family when we went outside, but they had gone.'

'So there were two bears?'

Linda smiled. 'Years later, Mum told me that the family had been speaking French, which was why Michael always faced south, as though he'd been waiting for his partner to come back from overseas.'

Rachel smiled. 'I don't think I've ever heard that story before.'

'Ah, your grandmother must have told you at some point. She was always one for looking back.' Linda smiled. 'Not like me. Always looking forward, wasn't I?'

'I think you've talked more about the past today than you did during my entire childhood,' Rachel said. She was joking, but from the way Linda gave barely a half-smile, she realised she was right. Forwards and onwards had always been Linda's motto. If you spent too much time looking back, you weren't looking where you were going.

'Well, what should we do with Michael,' Linda said, letting her hair fall over her eyes. 'We can't just give him to a charity shop, can we? Not while he's still waiting.'

'No. No, we can't.'

Linda brushed her hair back and looked up. Her eyes looked filmy, as though she were holding back tears. 'Shall we have another coffee?'

'Yes,' Rachel said. 'I think that's a good idea.'

∽

With coffee breaks every half an hour or so, it was unlikely Rachel would be able to sleep for several days, but the sheer weight of the memories unearthed as they went through Grandma Marigold's things meant her mind would be buzzing too much anyway. There were the little china houses Rachel had begun to give her grandmother for Christmas once she was getting pocket money. Then there was a picture of herself and the kids who had once lived next door to Grandma—Sally and Wayne—the day they'd had a bicycle race down to the village, up the other side of the valley and then around in a circle via Smuggler's Lane, a narrow, twisting road that cut across the river via a stone arched bridge and then up the back of the valley behind a row of converted wheel houses. The three of them, triumphant, stood with their bikes at the top of the hill, with Porth Melynos in the background. The photo had stood for years on Grandma's shelf in the dining room, watching over them as they ate Sunday lunch.

'When did they move away?' Rachel asked. 'I remember playing with them for years, then one day they just kind of dropped out of our lives.'

'Wayne was a year younger than you, Sally two,' Linda said. 'So when you went to secondary school, you kind of outgrew them really fast. You didn't want to play with them anymore. They were still there for another year or so, but then they moved up to London. Once you started getting homework, we stopped going over to Mum's so much, so we didn't really see them. Mum said they always asked after you.'

'I wonder what happened to them?'

'Their family name was Luton, so you could look them up online.'

Rachel nodded. She wanted to, and she didn't. Sometimes it was better to leave the memories as they were, in sepia, their edges faded. Dragging them kicking and screaming into the cold light of day could only ruin them, dilute them with the harshness of now.

'Oh, gosh, look at these,' Linda said, lifting up an

ancient photograph album and opening the front cover. These go way back, probably to wartime. Mum probably got these from Grandma Mary, your great grandmother.'

Linda began to carefully turn the pages. Rachel caught glimpses of faded portrait photos, a couple of panoramic views of the village with far fewer buildings, some pictures of a proud-looking man holding a terrier on a lead.

'That's your great grandfather,' she said. 'Benjamin Castle. He went over to France and never came back. Grandma Mary lived with some cousins after that, until her own mother died and left her this house.'

'She never remarried?'

Linda shook her head. 'No. She only ever talked about Grandpa Benjamin, what a great man he was and all that. They were in love, she said. No one could have replaced him.'

'It must have been hard for Grandma Marigold to grow up without a father,' Rachel said, before she was fully aware of the words coming out of her mouth. As soon as the look on Linda's face made the connotation clear, she clapped a hand over her mouth, then mumbled, 'So … it's been at least half an hour since the last coffee, so I think we need another one.'

Linda nodded. 'I was thinking the same thing.'

∼

They got little done for the rest of the day, with Linda calling a halt just after three o'clock to give herself time to go home and get ready for her evening shift in The Harbour View Hotel. She gave Rachel a lift down the hill, but Rachel, feeling a little overawed by the weight of layered memories, asked to be let out by the harbour. As Linda drove off, Rachel walked out to the end of the breakwater and sat down with her feet over the edge, watching the narrow inlet and the sea water sloshing at the weed covered rocks below.

From here, the open sea was hidden, but she could see the entire village, nestled into the valley's steep V. It looked as photo-friendly as ever, but Rachel was already starting to feel like she no longer belonged here. Most of her friends had done the same as her, gone off to university and not come back, some even scattering across the globe. With the exception of Gavin, she had never been close to the people who had stuck around, taking up practical trades or segueing seamlessly into family-run businesses.

Some people, like Mrs. Simcock and her sister Clara, craved the peace and quiet by the sea, but when you were older, your priorities changed. Rachel could appreciate Porth Melynos for a few days, but to live here again? No chance. The only good thing about Grandma's death was that one more connection to the village was gone, and Rachel was almost set free.

Or was that set adrift? Perhaps she was no more than an uprooted tree, floating aimlessly down a long, meandering river. What was coming? A waterfall, or a saw mill?

Across the harbour, the lights in the Horse and Buoy Inn had just come on. Rachel had learned her lesson about leaving her purse at home, and now carried it in her jeans' pocket. With a smile, she stood up, and went to get a pint.

5

THE FISHERMAN

'If there's anything you want, whether it's practical or sentimental, just let me know,' Linda said, as they carried an old, tatty sideboard outside and lowered it into the small car trailer Linda had borrowed from a friend at work. 'I'll be taking a few bits and bobs, but we can't keep everything. A lot of this furniture is just junk.'

Rachel agreed in principle, but it was still hard to let go. On one end of the sideboard was a scrawled picture in black marker that was supposedly Snoopy, drawn by herself circa age seven. Grandma Marigold had been horrified—despite praising Rachel's fledgling artistic skills—and had repositioned the sideboard so that the defaced side was now hidden by the wall. Rachel had forgotten all about it until they had pulled it out.

'I really don't think you should sell,' she said. 'What about when you retire in a couple of years? You won't have to walk down the hill to the hotel every night then. You can just sit and look out of the window.'

'And wait to die?' Linda sighed. 'I'm sorry. It's just that I don't really know what to do with this place. I suppose I could just rent it out. This area is popular, and there's not much available. I just don't think I could handle someone else living here.'

'But that's what'll happen if you sell it.'

'But I won't need to think of it as mine, then,' Linda said. 'I can just forget about it. Look, I'll think about whether to rent it or put it up for sale. I just don't know right now.'

Rachel struggled to understand her mother's logic, but Linda was still struggling with her grief. Grandma Marigold, in Rachel's absence, had been Linda's only local-living family. She had no brothers or sisters, and Grandpa Trevor, like Great Grandpa Benjamin, had continued a Castle tradition for male members of the family by dying young, before Linda was born. That the ongoing fatherless, only-daughter, bloodline of the Castle family had continued into her own generation, wasn't lost on Rachel, but it was best not to dwell on it. The only thing she had managed to figure out was that Castle had been neither her mother's nor grandmother's married name, both reverting to the family name upon widowhood or abandonment. She had always wondered whether her father's family name had been something weird like Von Crappershufflebotham, in which case, Castle did just fine.

'So, this stuff is for the dump?' Rachel asked.

Linda gave a reluctant nod. 'Are you good with taking it up? I put you on my car insurance, remember? I'll stay here and go through a few more boxes.'

Rachel nodded, and took her mother's keys. The ongoing nostalgia was starting to drive her round the twist, so it felt good to get out of the village for a while, even if it was only to go to the local council dump, where she offloaded the old and broken furniture from the trailer, touching each piece with a lingering tenderness that felt like a last goodbye. She felt bad about wanting to go back to Brentwell, but Grandma's death meant her mother was the only string keeping her here. Perhaps, if Linda sold the house, Rachel could convince her to buy a little place closer to Brentwell, and they could close down the Castle family connection with Sunset Harbour forever.

She paused, a cardboard box of old dinner trays in her hand, their images cracked and faded. *What am I thinking? Why do I want so much to let go?*

Shaking her head, she had to force her arms to move, throwing the box over the edge, where the trays scattered among other discarded junk, much of it now rain-damaged and broken. A few more boxes later, the trailer was empty, and she headed back to the village. When she got back to Grandma's place, however, Linda had left a note taped to the door.

Mrs. Green from Number 17 popped by and invited me for a coffee. If you want to join us, please come along. If not, don't worry. I'll see you in a bit.

Mrs. Green was an old busybody whom Linda had an unexplainable liking for, perhaps because Mrs. Green could fill even the shortest of silences with some nugget of local gossip scraped from the walls of her many social clubs and events. Linda had once joked that it was like watching a variety show live on air, but Rachel had never seen the appeal. Instead, she went into Grandma's house, made herself a coffee, and sat at the window, looking out on the view of Sunset Harbour she had seen so many times that she could still recall even the tiniest details at will. The flowerbed in the garden of the Seafront Hotel, speckled with red and orange tulips in spring, pink and yellow roses in summer. The spinning washing line at

Hawker's Cottage across the valley, which had seemingly survived countless winter storms still with its spininess intact. The broken window on the second floor on the landward side of the Horse and Buoy Inn, one that she remembered getting broken when she was in primary school by a group of boys playing cricket in the car park. Local legend had it that the boy's dad had bought the landlord a case of whisky in lieu of money for a replacement, and a piece of tape had been enough ever since.

All right, she thought with a smile, she couldn't actually see the crack from here, but she could see the window, and she'd seen the crack when she had walked past the other day, so she knew it was still there.

From the window, the breakwater was also visible. A large concrete right angle, on the landward side was the little harbour, while on the other was a choppy inlet about thirty metres across, which was great for swimming and even snorkeling on a calm day, or for fishing the rest of the time. In the summer, local kids would swim across from the breakwater and climb a little way up the cliff on the other side via a couple of natural staircases and then throw themselves off into the water, the higher the better. A couple of the most popular spots even had names handed down over a couple of generations: Little Poke, because it wasn't very high and only poked a little way out into the water, then a bit higher was Gaggers, because it supposedly took a few goes to get up the nerve, and a gag was required to hold back the screams.

And finally, the highest spot that could be safely climbed to, nearly ten metres above the water, was Knacker's Point, one that few kids had been brave enough to try during Rachel's schooldays, but which had apparently been popular back in Grandma Marigold's youth, supposedly because there was no TV, electricity, or any other modern distraction. Knacker's Point had become a bit of a rite of passage for young men in the village, in particular the tougher types, Grandma had often said, but had also caused a dearth in local fertility rates, because, in Grandma Marigold's words, 'If the wind pulled your legs too far apart on the way down, it would squish those little things like a pair of Maltesers left on the tracks at Bodmin Parkway station.'

Rachel smiled at the memory, even if at the time, she hadn't really understood. And while Grandma had always claimed the declining birthrate was a direct result of a lack of working knackers in the local area, Rachel preferred to go with the more commonly accepted idea, that it was due to an aging population.

There was a pair of binoculars on the windowsill, where Grandma had always kept them. Rachel leaned over and picked them up, wiping a little dust off the eye pieces before lifting them to her face. With a smile, she scanned the village below, watching a few late season tourists wandering along the harbourside, in and out of the cafés and shops. Moving her view slowly down to the breakwater, she scanned the greenish water and the silty patch of sand which was the village's only attempt at a beach, and even then only at low tide. Up on the breakwater, which also served as the harbour wall, a handful of fishermen sat on deckchairs, their rods protruding out to sea. She recognised one of them as an old school friend's dad from his jacket and the way his hat sat at a slight angle, but the others were all facing away from her, their identities unknown.

All except one, who sat facing the other way, his rod angling out over the water below the breakwater on the inward side.

'Catch nothing down there but a cold,' she remembered an elderly local called Jiminy Dent had told her and some friends once, when, as children of no older than eight or nine, they and taken their tourist shop-bought rods and dangled the nylon line in the water. 'Maybe crabs, but you'll get them a lot quicker down Plymouth Hoe on a Friday night.'

Rachel still remembered his cackling laughter as he wandered off, at the time assuming he was referring to some fishmonger of which he was a frequent customer. By the time she had realised, years later, old Jiminy had been lying under the soil in St. Lancel's churchyard for nearly a decade, having ironically fallen off the breakwater one windy winter's day and drowned.

The fisherman facing her was unfamiliar. In fact, as Rachel held the binoculars steady to get a clear view of him, he didn't look like either a local or a proper fisherman at all. He was young, probably in his late twenties, and beneath a light windcheater he wore a black sweater and jeans. Rachel tried to focus on his face, but couldn't seem to get a clear view. He was shifting around a lot, despite being seated.

In fact, he appeared to be speaking to someone.

Rachel frowned. It was common these days to see people speaking to themselves as they walked up the street, chattering via a headset so small as to be nearly invisible. Down in the valley, however, it was almost impossible to get a signal, and out on the breakwater you would be too far away from any of the hotels or cafés which had wi-fi.

Rachel smiled. It was almost comforting to know that the man—who was fairly easy on the eye when she was able to hold the binoculars steady enough—was a fruit loop.

There was something else that reinforced the idea, too.

In a brief moment where both her binoculars and the man had been still enough to give her a photograph-perfect view, she had discovered that it would be quite impossible for him to catch anything.

He was fishing without any line.

6
NO WAY OUT

September storms weren't uncommon, but they usually didn't kick off until later in the month. As Rachel stared at the rain battering her mother's living room window, she wondered if perhaps she shouldn't stay an extra day.

'What's a job interview anyway?' Linda said, making one last cup of tea with a morose look in her eyes that made Rachel feel like she was heading off to war. 'You're young, bright, educated … there'll be many more, won't there?'

'Mum….'

Linda sighed. 'I just wish you'd stay a little longer, that's all. You hardly ever visit these days, and if Grandma hadn't died, you probably wouldn't be here now.'

'I'll come down at Christmas.'

'You only live an hour and an half away. You could come down again next Saturday.'

Rachel knew she was fighting a losing battle, and part of her was churning up with guilt. Her mother was totally right, but there was something about Porth Melynos that left Rachel feeling weird inside. Like by being here she was showing how little she'd achieved in life. Like the benchmark for success in this village was to no longer live in it. Then there were the memories and the suffocating nostalgia—

'I'll try to come down again in a couple of weeks,' Rachel said, hoping the compromise would pacify her mother. As Linda brought over the final cup of tea and set it down with a soft thunk on the coaster, Rachel saw the defeat in her mother's eyes.

'You do what you feel is best,' Linda said. 'And I suppose I'll just have to deal with it, won't I?'

∾

Twenty minutes and a few tears later, she was pulling out into the road as rain lashed against her windscreen and wind ragged the hedgerows, sending handfuls of displaced leaves billowing through the air. Linda had thankfully not come down to see her off, so, wiping her last tears away, Rachel headed up the road leading out of the valley. In half an hour or so she'd be out of the maze of lanes and into open country, and with a little luck with traffic, she'd be home by lunchtime, drinking a cup of coffee in Bethany's flat, thinking about what she could do tomorrow afternoon, once the dreaded job interview was over.

And then, like a sudden whirlwind, all the fears came rushing in. She was unemployed, rent was due in a couple of weeks, and she had no prospects on the horizon other than another poorly paid temping job tapping numbers into a screen for some company of which she'd never heard. The car, already starting to wheeze a little, needed servicing in November, and she'd been a little too loose with her credit card in the last few weeks. It felt like strong hands closing in around her, ready to squeeze her like a lemon until there was nothing but a bit of crushed pulp left.

She thumped the steering wheel in frustration, even as the sheeting rain blinded her view of the road ahead. One of her wipers had come loose, and was no longer actually scraping the rain away, so she got a brief second of clarity on the passenger side before she was blinded once again. She slowed the car to a crawl, hoping the rain would ease, but it only seemed to get harder, tormenting her. The wind, too, was buffeting the little Fiesta, rocking it from side to side.

And then, like a sudden finishing move, a line of darkness fell across her vision. A loud crunch preceded her car bumping upwards, her seatbelt locking, and the airbag pluming, filling her vision even as the windscreen shattered. For a moment there was only a breathless silence, then the whole world rushed in, the wind wrapped around her, the rain lashed her face, and something massive and gnarly and dark brown was lying across the crushed front of her car, filling her nostrils with the pungent scent of moss and soggy leaves.

∽

'Well,' Linda said, sitting beside Rachel in the hospital waiting room, sounding just a little smug as she picked at a fingernail. 'I suppose I could drive you back up to Brentwell now that the storm's relented, but who would look after you? You can't expect Bethany to wait on you hand and foot. She's got her own work to do.'

Rachel grimaced. It felt like her mother was actually a witch who had commanded the old tree to come crashing down. 'I broke one small bone in my foot and they put me in a cast,' she said with a sigh. 'And I only broke that because the fireman dropped his cutter when they were levering me out.'

'He slipped in the rain,' Linda said. 'He must have apologised a thousand times, the poor man. They were just so desperate to get you out in case the tree shifted or another one came down. It broke a power line, you know. The power's still out.'

'That's too bad. I hope it won't take long to fix.'

'Colin said probably by this evening.'

'Colin?'

'The fireman.'

'Oh, you're on first name terms, are you?' Rachel couldn't resist a tired smile.

Linda's cheeks reddened. 'Actually, Colin and me … he asked me out for dinner.'

Rachel stared. 'Aren't you—'

'—a bit old for a toyboy?' Linda laughed. 'Colin's sixty-four. He's actually retired, but a retained firefighter, kind of like a reserve in case there aren't enough on duty and there's a great big disaster. They had to send the volunteers out to you because all the downed power lines meant they were short staffed.'

'I'm not sure whether to feel worse about that or better because I'm saving tax payer's money,' Rachel said. 'Although I'd have saved a lot more if they hadn't bothered with this cast,' she added, tapping the fresh lump of white plaster on the floor tiles. 'They could have just given me a padded sock or something.'

The door opened, and a doctor came out of his office. He glanced at a clipboard and then looked up with a smile.

'Ms Castle? You're free to go home now. Make sure you get plenty of rest. Come back again in two weeks and we'll have another look, see if we can take that cast off. You're a lucky girl.'

My car's totaled, I'm stuck on crutches for at least two weeks, and I now have to put up with my mother waiting on me.

'Thanks,' she said with a grim smile.

As the doctor smiled and went out, Linda patted Rachel on the arm. 'Oh, there's one more thing I forgot to tell you. Colin is Cathy Ubbers's dad. You remember Cathy from school, don't you?'

Rachel briefly wished the tree had fallen on her head.

'How could I forget?' she said.

∽

'Why can't I stay in Grandma's house? The views are better, and I can sit at the window and drink coffee until I start to shake.'

'The doctor told you to take some exercise, and from there you've only got up and down,' Linda said, helping Rachel out of the car and up the path. 'And what if you want to hobble down to the shops? At least it's all flat here.'

'Except for the stairs,' Rachel said as Linda opened the front door, revealing the narrow set of stairs that led up to her mother's first floor flat.

'Ah, you'll get used to those,' Linda said. 'Go on, up you go. I'll wait down here to catch you if you have any trouble.'

'You're enjoying this, aren't you?' Rachel grumbled, lodging herself into the doorway and starting up, her underarms already aching from the crutches.

'Well, it'll be nice to have someone to chat with for once,' Linda said. 'I can move your bed closer to the window if you like. I know you can't see anything much except the road, but it's better than nothing.'

'I'm not exactly bedridden,' Rachel said. 'It's one small bone.'

'Yes, but you still need to rest.'

'I can rest at night. By day I'd be happier with an armchair and a stool, if you must insist.'

'Yes, that'll be nice. Then we can sit and chat over tea and biscuits. I can tell you all about my dates with Colin.'

Rachel grimaced. 'Actually, if you could move the bed, that would be great.'

∼

The sudden September storm that had left the power off for two days, blown down half a dozen trees and sent numerous roof tiles flying into the road, was gone as quickly as it had come. Two days after her forced incarceration had begun, the sun was shining in a pleasant autumn sky, and it felt as though nothing had happened.

Linda had gone back up to Grandma's to continue clearing things out, so Rachel decided to break her isolation and hobble down to the harbourside. The phone lines were down, and Linda's flat, tucked up against the steep hillside, had no mobile signal.

She had called Bethany from the hospital, but really needed to speak to her flatmate again, let her know a time frame for when she might return, and beg for an extension on the rent.

Even though she had been practicing with the crutches around the flat, it was still a massive hassle to get down the stairs, and her armpits ached like someone had hit them with a hammer. Even though she'd wrapped and taped old hand towels around the hard plastic lumps, she still found herself wincing with each awkward step.

As she struggled down the road to the harbour, young

people ignored her while older people muttered quiet hellos and offered knowing nods as though identifying with her predicament. Rachel wanted to scream 'It's one tiny bone!' but resisted, mainly because being considered crazy in addition to being invalid was unlikely to improve her day.

Eventually, however, she made it as far as the harbourside and slumped down on a bench to rest. It was a fine day, with the sun shining gloriously—almost mockingly—in the sky, the breeze up the valley crisp on her skin, the colours on the headlands starting to fade from green to brown.

Rachel pulled her phone out of her pocket. She had one bar of signal, but when she tried to call, the bar swiftly disappeared. A couple of the cafés had wi-fi, but she had neglected to bring her purse and would feel compelled to buy something. Instead, she stood up again, and began to hobble in the direction of the slipway leading down onto the tiny triangle of beach revealed by the retreated tide.

Pausing at the top to check, she found she had two bars of signal, but the second was wavering in and out. She needed a little more to be certain the call would connect. She hobbled on down the slipway and out onto the gravelly sand, angling towards the moored boats in the water. Checking once more, she now had two solid bars, a third flickering on and off.

A few more steps and she was out of sight of tourists walking along the breakwater, a moored fishing boat between them. Rachel leaned on her crutches, pulling out her phone again, and pulled up Bethany's number. To her delight, it began to ring.

'Rachel? Is that you? Sorry, I can't talk long, I'm at work.'

Rachel almost cried out with relief. 'Yeah, it's me,' she said. 'Sorry—'

'I've been trying to get hold of you,' Bethany said, interrupting her. 'I have some news—'

'What's happened?'

'Look … I'm not sure how to say this, but Matt asked me to marry him.'

'No!'

'Yes!'

'Congratulations!'

'Thanks.'

'We'll open a bottle of champagne when I get back next week—'

'About that … ah, I have some other news.'

The breeze tickled around Rachel's neck, and she felt certain she was sinking. 'What news?'

'I was talking to a guy at work, and he told me he had a friend looking for a flat in the area, and you know, since Matt said I could live with him, and this guy came around and had a look, and … and….'

It was only lunchtime, but the sun appeared to be setting.

'What happened?' Rachel thought she asked, but she couldn't be sure, as her ears were filled with white noise.

'Well, he made me an offer on the flat. And I accepted. It was too much not to, and you know, well, I'm going to go and live at Matt's place, and—'

'So I'm homeless?'

'Well, no, because you're living at your mum's, aren't you?'

'But my room—'

'I felt bad, so I've refunded your last month's rent, and I've paid back all your deposit. I had to clear out your stuff because the guy wants to move in this weekend, but I'm happy to courier it down to your mum's place. It's the least I can do.'

Rachel dropped her phone. It landed with a soft splat on wet sand.

'Rachel?' came a faint voice. 'Are you all right? Listen, I've got to go. Speak soon, okay?'

Bethany hung up without waiting for an answer, and Rachel's phone screen went back to its default picture, of the two of them sitting in a café in Brentwell's Sycamore Park, a pair of large, froth-covered lattes in front of them.

Good days, now a memory.

Feeling like the sky—or at least she—was falling, Rachel leaned down to pick up her phone … and realised it was far closer than it should have been.

'Wha…?'

As she grabbed her phone, her crutches had sunk into the sand. She tried to pull one free, but a sudden jolt of pain raced up her leg as she put her weight on the cast.

That one small broken bone was certainly making itself felt.

'Uh … help?' she muttered, looking around, but there was no one nearby, the fishing boats bobbing gently but emptily in the water. She glanced behind her at the tide line further up the beach, aware that at high tide all the sand was covered. To her relief, it wasn't that high; she would still have her head and shoulders above water.

So, she wouldn't drown, just be humiliated.

'Are you all right down there?'

She looked up to see someone standing on the breakwater, peering between the nearest fishing boats. It was a young man who looked vaguely familiar.

The fisherman she had spied on from Grandma's window, the one without the line.

'Ah, I'm a little stuck,' Rachel muttered, feeling heat bloom into her cheeks.

'Just wait a minute. I'll come and get you out.'

Before Rachel could answer, he had set down his lineless rod and was hurrying back around the breakwater. As he came back into sight around the fishing boats, Rachel had a few seconds to study him before he jumped down on to the slipway.

With a green-grey waxed jacket, Wellington boots, and a woolly, unkempt hat despite the seasonally pleasant weather, he looked like he had copied the picture off the front of a fishing magazine. He was the perfect stereotype aside from one thing: he didn't appear interested in the actual fish.

'Wow, looks like you got caught in a squishy patch,' he said as he jogged up to her. He was younger than she had first thought when watching him from Grandma's window, perhaps in his mid to late twenties. He had a wisp of beard and hair that needed a cut poking awkwardly out from under his hat, but bright blue eyes the same colour as the autumn sky.

'I didn't realise,' Rachel said.

'What were you doing down here, anyway?' he said, as he reached out and gave one of the crutches a jostle until it came loose with a squelchy pop. 'Interested in the boats?'

Rachel shrugged. 'I was trying to get a phone signal.'

'Why didn't you just walk out on the breakwater? It works fine out there. Half those old guys are listening to radio shows on their phones.'

Why hadn't she just walked out along the breakwater? It was flat and wide enough not to cause any problems. Rachel could only give a dumb shrug as the man tugged her other crutch free.

'What happened to your foot?'

Feeling a little spiky to hide her embarrassment, Rachel said, 'I broke it, obviously.' Immediately regretting her spikiness, she tried to soften it by adding, 'Only one small bone, though.'

'Sorry to hear that,' the man said, although his own tone suggested he was a little offended. 'Let me help you back up to the harbourside.'

'I can manage,' Rachel said, her mouth reacting faster than her brain. The man, however, took her on her word and backed off a couple of steps.

'Well, just take it slowly, and watch out for those rocks over there. And that green seaweed is slippery.'

Rachel, seemingly unable to close the floodgates now that they were open, said, 'I grew up here. So I know.'

The man shrugged again, but this time said nothing until they got to the foot of the concrete slipway. 'Are you all right getting up here?' he said, but in a tone that suggested he had already predicted the answer.

Rachel could hardly request his assistance now. 'I'll be fine,' she said.

'No problem.'

He walked alongside her until they were back up on the flat, then gave her a shy smile. 'My name's William,' he said.

Rachel nodded. Her tongue was being a little devil, and she found herself saying, 'Thanks for looking out for me. I'll be okay from here,' when really, she wanted to ask what he was doing down here on the breakwater, why he was fishing without using any line, and even more importantly, to tell him her name.

He smiled, offered a little wave, and backed off slowly, as though to pacify an angry bear. As soon as he felt a safe distance away, he turned and walked off, head down, not looking back. Rachel watched him go, hoping he would glance back over his shoulder. When he reached his fishing gear, he picked up his rod, dangled it over the edge of the breakwater, and sat down with his back to her, leaving Rachel to stump back up the road, homeless, broken, and lonelier in the world than she could ever remember being before.

7

ROSE COLOURED DAYS

'I WAS TALKING TO CLARA IN THE FUDGE SHOP THIS morning,' Linda said, setting down a tray on which sat a steaming cup of tea and a plate topped with fudge which she had presumably just bought. 'She said they're unseasonably busy at the moment, so if you want, she can give you a few part time hours. Plus, she quite often has to go up to Brentwell on other business, so Valerie would need some help.'

Rachel stared out of the window at the street. One hand reached for the tea on autopilot, because it was one of two things the days being cared for by Linda had taught her. The other was getting into and out of the cramped toilet without either getting stuck, hurt, or wet.

Cause and effect. It was like a lot of things. The constant, endless cups of tea caused the … well, it didn't need to be dwelled on. Rachel's departure for university had been the cause for Gavin falling into Cathy Ubbers' sizable encompassing arms, and perhaps Rachel being an inherently bad person in some way she didn't quite understand was the cause for losing both her car and flat, and indeed her way in life, to the point that she was getting offered summer jobs for students in the middle of autumn.

'Rachel? Are you in there? My little girl's still the daydreamer, I see.'

'Sorry, I was just thinking about how my life sucks. Thanks for the tea.'

'Don't be too down on yourself,' Linda said, sitting down across the table. 'These things happen. Perhaps next month you'll get a run of good luck.'

'I wouldn't count on it.' Rachel frowned. 'Mum … do you think I'm pretty?'

Linda grinned. 'My dear, of course I do. You're the prettiest girl in the world.'

Rachel felt her cheeks redden. 'Thanks, Mum. But you have to say that, don't you, because you're my mum. How would you answer if you were say, Cathy's mum?'

Linda pursed her lips. 'Well … I suppose that would depend on whether I was saying it in public or private. If it was in private, of course I'd say you were pretty, because you are, but if I was say, talking to Cathy, I'd probably say you were a dog, just to make her feel better.'

Rachel gave a horrified gasp. 'So I'm a dog?'

'No, I'm just saying that Melanie Ubbers might call you a dog, in order to make Cathy feel better. Bless her, she's lively and all, but she's no oil painting.'

'That's not very nice.'

'Even though you agree.'

'I didn't say she was a dog, you said I was a dog.'

Linda laughed. 'No, I said Melanie Ubbers would say you're a dog in certain circumstances, but to be honest, it doesn't really matter because she's blind in one eye, and can only see half of you at a time.'

'Is that supposed to be a joke? Or is Cathy's mum really blind in one eye?'

Linda laughed again. 'Both.'

'Really?'

'Yeah, I was there when it happened. We were on detention for getting caught smoking behind the old minibus they had in those days at the back of the teachers' car park, and we were doing gardening in the little shrubbery area around by the office entrance, and Melanie stepped on a rake that was lying on the floor and the pole smacked her in the eye.'

'Wait a minute … way too much to digest there. You used to smoke?'

Linda shrugged. 'Only the odd one. In those days you had to because all the cool boys did. And Melanie's mum worked in a bookies so she'd always steal them off the punters, and Melanie would steal them off her. I was only mates with her for the fags.'

'Um … right. And the rake?'

'Nailed her right in the left eye. Didn't poke it out, but it left her blind, or something they call it these days, visually challenged, or whatever. It's still in there, but she wears a contact so you can't tell. Next time you see her, have a good look at it. It doesn't move quite like the other one because the muscles have gone lazy over time.'

'Wasn't there a bit of a fallout?'

'Oh, yeah. The school got done for health and safety, the headmaster got sacked. All detentions had to be done in the classroom after that. They were no fun anymore, and it was all because Melanie Ubbers was stupid enough to step on a rake.'

Rachel smiled as she shook her head. 'Why couldn't you have told me this when I was fourteen? I could have done with a bit of ammunition.'

'You never asked me if Cathy's mum would call you pretty.'

Rachel laughed. 'My mistake.'

'So, are you going to take that job or not? Since you're going to be stuck here for a little longer than planned?'

'Is there anywhere else in the village that's hiring?'

Linda smiled. 'I saw a note in the window of the launderette a couple of days ago. They're understaffed. Too many tourists and not enough washer-dryers in those holiday lets. I'll be seeing Melanie at W.I. on Tuesday so if you want I can look her in the one functioning eye and put a good word in for you.'

Rachel wrinkled her nose. 'I think I'll go with the fudge. Anyway, knowing Cathy, she'd make me put in an application, just to complete the humiliation.'

Linda leaned forward. 'You know, you should maybe give her another chance. She might still look like the same bulldozer she was when you were at school, but she's softened up a little, and I don't mean round the waist.'

Rachel started to laugh. 'Mum, you're so funny. Sometimes I just can't understand why—'

She managed to stop herself before she said what had been unofficially forbidden to be said in her mother's presence for as long as she could remember.

Why Dad left.

Instead, she forced a smile, grabbed a bit of fudge, and stuffed it into her mouth. 'Just in case Clara gives me a flavour test,' she blathered, aware she was doing a pretty terrible job of covering her tracks. Linda's eyes told her the damage was already done, but her mother gamely took a sip of her own tea, then stood up, muttering something about washing to put on. She turned away, but too slowly, and Rachel caught a glimpse of a tear rolling down her cheek before Linda's back was to her, and moving swiftly away, like an ocean liner departing from port, still visible, but already gone, already untouchable.

8

SPORTING UNDERACHIEVER

CLARA, STANDING BY THE DOOR WITH HER BAG OVER HER shoulder and a hat protecting her greying but elegant head, smiled a fairy godmother smile as she prepared to leave Rachel to the wiles of the wicked witch.

'Valerie will show you everything you need to know,' she said. 'I'll be back in a few days to see how you've got on. Good luck, and we really appreciate it, especially since you still have to deal with that cast.'

Rachel forced a smile, but inside she was churning with dread, aware of the dark shadow at her shoulder that was Mrs. Simcock, holding a wooden spoon in one hand and beating it into the other like a drummer serenading an execution. The bell tinkled as Clara went out, and with sweat trickling down her forehead, Rachel turned to face her doom.

'Did you hear the one about the confectionary who failed an exam?' Mrs. Simcock said, face poker straight.

'Er … no,' Rachel muttered.

'He fudged it. Ha!'

Mrs. Simcock's explosion of laughter was so loud that

Rachel stumbled backwards, bumping against the glass display case on top of the counter and causing a dangerous rattle. As she let out a gasp of fear, her heart racing, Mrs. Simcock slapped the wooden spoon into her hand three times and gave a nightmarish grin.

'Come on, dear, have a laugh with an old crone like me.'

Then, before Rachel could even respond, she had turned and gone back into the kitchen, leaving Rachel alone in the empty shop, with only a display case piled high with delicious-smelling fudge for company.

The urge to comfort eat had never been greater.

∼

She wasn't expected to do much more than stand behind the counter and serve the occasional customer. As well as fudge and a few varieties of coffee, the shop sold the usual tourist fare: postcards, tea towels, calendars, and trinkets made out of shells, but not so much, so Valerie said, 'as to get us into a gangland war with one of those tat specialists down by the harbour.'

Valerie. After a couple of hours of maintaining the tyrant charade, Valerie had insisted on them being on first name terms, and almost at once Rachel began to let go of the old pupil-teacher fear she had held onto since her early teens. While never quite losing the snarling, fear-inducing persona that had likely terrified pupils of her science classes both long before and after Rachel's brief internment, Valerie had a dry sense of humour and a dark wit that at times had Rachel in stitches, and at other times struggling to maintain a straight face in the onslaught of suppressed laughter moments after Valerie had dropped a comment about an incoming customer before vanishing into the kitchen.

'That man just about to come in is wearing a toupee. I'll give you a five pound bonus if you wait until he's seated then go over and ask if he'd like you to turn down the ceiling fan.'

Thankfully, the man had ordered his fudge and coffee for takeaway, but not looking at a bouncing section of his hair for the five minutes she was serving him showed a level of restraint and dedication for which the Shaolin Monks would be proud.

In fact, a couple of days into her new job, Rachel found she was actually enjoying herself. The job was far from taxing, and while Sunset Harbour Coffee and Fudge Company had a handful of customers over lunchtime, most of the time it wasn't busy. Valerie always had an anecdote from her teaching days to share, but when she was busy in the kitchen she was happy enough for Rachel to read a book or magazine if there was nothing she needed to do.

'Just don't fall asleep and put your head through the display glass. But, if you do, and you get blood on the fudge, just tell the customers it's cranberry.'

As the days began to drift past, however, September crawling slowly towards October with a gust of chill wind and the gentle browning of the hillsides, the inevitable began to happen: the tourist numbers dried up, and more and more often Rachel found herself having to deal with the locals.

∼

She was reading a Jack Benton paperback one morning when the bell over the door tingled and she looked up to see a 2022 vintage of a woman she hadn't seen since the glorious London Olympics year of 2012, when, buoyed up by all the sports on television, a thirteen-year-old Rachel had been inspired to join the village hall's badminton club.

Maureen Grover, bank clerk in Plymouth by day but former Olympic-trials badminton player by now distant memory, cocked her head and smiled at the girl she had briefly coached, before Rachel had got bored around the six-week mark and given up.

'Rachel Castle, is that you? I heard from a friend of your mother's that you'd moved back to the village. I'm guessing city life didn't agree with you?'

Only the bumpkinest of country bumpkins would refer to Brentwell as a city, but Rachel nodded and gave a shy smile.

'A series of unfortunate events,' she said.

'Ah, but you're still young. There's time left for you to escape. I never thought we'd see you around here again, though. Anyone with anything about them gets out as soon as they can.'

The kitchen door creaked, and Rachel glanced back to see Valerie standing there, out of sight of Maureen, a finger hooked inside her mouth and a grin on her face as she tugged on the inside of her cheek. Turning back, Rachel said, 'I'm only back temporarily.'

'Ah, I said that once,' Maureen said. 'Mind you, at least I escape by day, if only to Plymouth. By the way, I'm still running the club, if you want another go. It looks like you could do with some exercise.'

Rachel gritted her teeth as Maureen looked pointedly at her midriff. She thought about attempting a roundhouse kick with her cast, but wasn't confident she could get it above knee height, and formerly nimble Maureen would likely delight at the chance to show her old speed around the court. Instead, Rachel just said, 'I'll give it some thought.'

'Well, don't think too long. You might still have a couple of years of A Team in you. Those worthless slobs in the B Team only do it for the after match drinks. Haven't won a match in three years.'

The idea of playing a game and then having a few drinks afterwards sounded perfect, but Maureen had such a glowering look on her face that Rachel could only give a stern nod and mutter, 'Infidels,' under her breath.

'Quite, quite,' Maureen said. 'I'll have two hundred grams of blueberry and three hundred of clotted cream and cookie.'

Rachel must have looked surprised at the substantial order, because Maureen chuckled and said, 'Bonuses come out next month, so best to get your bribes in with the boss early. You don't think I'd be seen dead eating this rubbish, do you?'

Out of the corner of her eye, Rachel caught sight of Valerie pretending to choke herself in the kitchen. She focused on a small mole in the centre of Maureen's forehead and smiled.

'Coming right up.'

As she turned away to grab a couple of bags, she hoped Maureen might consider their conversation over, but her old coach was just going through some warm ups.

'Do you have a boyfriend these days?' she said, as Rachel began to scoop fudge into a bag. 'I mean, I remember you were with that Gavin lad in school, but you're obviously not with him anymore, are you? He's with Catherine Ubbers, so I see. He's not keeping you on the backburner, is he?'

'No,' Rachel said.

'Well, my nephew, Lawrence, he's still single. Want me to put a good word in for you?'

'Ah, no, I'll be okay,' Rachel said, feeling her cheeks redden as, in the kitchen, Valerie pretended to put a metal pan over her head and bang on it with her wooden spoon.

'He's not that bad. I mean, he does smell a bit, but he's a fishmonger, what do you expect? And he renovated his flat last year so it's not as retro as it was. I know he's divorced, and he's over forty, but he's still quite a catch—'

Valerie slipped, banging the pan with the spoon and then nearly tripping over. Rachel could see her mouth twisted up with laughter, but with the top of her head covered she just looked like an escaped mental patient.

'Sounds like you've got something going on in there,' Maureen said, leaning forward over the counter.

'Oh, it's nothing,' Rachel said quickly. 'I think we left a window open. Sea winds and all that.'

'Well, I'd better get back. See you again, I imagine.' Maureen leaned forward and winked. 'Next bonus season, most like.'

Rachel let out a long sigh as the door closed, the bell giving a little goodbye tinkle as Maureen Grover marched off up the street in the direction of the council car park. Rachel watched until she was out of sight then turned away, letting out a gasp when she found Valerie standing right at her shoulder, hands on hips.

'That must have been a nightmare.'

Rachel grimaced. 'I suppose I've got to get used to it.'

'Gradually, is usually best,' Valerie said. 'Why don't you grab some coffee and a bit of that old fudge and knock off early? We're not inundated and it looks like the sea mist is coming in. Plus, I don't want to work you off your … ah, foot.'

'Thanks.'

Rachel took a paper cup and a bag of fudge that Valerie had said was 'just to the on side of off', and headed out. As soon as she was out on the street however, hobbling with the crutch under one arm, the fudge and coffee held in her free hand, she didn't feel like going home. Her mum wouldn't have started work yet and Rachel didn't feel like talking to anyone. Instead, she headed for the harbour.

Valerie had been right about the sea mist. By the time Rachel reached the harbourside, the sea mist had obscured the cliffs, leaving the breakwater as effectively the edge of the world. She had always liked to sit down on the beach but after sinking in last time, this time she didn't dare. Her mobility was getting better—she was down to using just one crutch—and the doctor had promised that the cast would come off next Monday. Rachel had tried to suggest an earlier date, but he had smiled one of those doctorly smiles, which was halfway between authoritarian and mocking, and told her it was better to be safe than sorry.

Unable to see much out in the harbour, she climbed the steps up on to the breakwater and hobbled out along the concrete strip to the right angle where it turned to protect the front of the harbour. The sea mist was so thick that she could see neither the end of the breakwater, nor the cliffs on the other side of the water, as though some god had stuffed a giant bung of cotton wool into the entire valley.

Vaguely aware that if she slipped and fell into the water, no one would likely see, but feeling defeatist enough anyway, Rachel turned and began to stump out towards the breakwater's far end.

She was halfway there when the mist gave up a shape: a figure sitting on a deckchair, hunched over a fishing rod.

William, the fisherman. He was facing inwards, his

line-less rod dangling out over the water. He looked up, eyes meeting hers.

Rachel froze. Caught in the horror grip of fate, the only choices remaining to her were to continue and engage him, or to make an obvious show of running—well, stumping—away. Her mind felt fogged by the mist and she clenched her fists, one over the crutch handle ... and felt the crinkle of the paper bag in the other.

The fudge. Perfect.

Feeling a surge of confidence, she moved again, inching forwards like a decommissioned cruise ship being towed into port.

'Ah, hello,' she said. 'Thanks for helping me out the other day. I brought you ... a thank you present.'

William wore a fisherman's jacket with a large hood that covered his eyes, but now he pushed it back, set down his rod, and stood up. He took a few steps towards her, a welcoming smile on his face.

'The quicksand girl,' he said.

Rachel would have blushed but the mist had left her cheeks damp and cold. 'To be fair,' she said, 'I don't think it was very quick. If you hadn't come, I'd have been in for a long, slow death.'

'I'm glad I was able to save you. Although I guess if I hadn't been able to get you out, I could have invoked a little entrepreneurialism and sold tickets.'

Rachel smiled. 'I doubt anyone would have paid to watch that.'

The fisherman shook his head. 'Certainly not. I've had needed to hire a balloon stall, maybe a magician as well. And organised helicopter tours.'

'You've got to think outside the box,' Rachel said.

The fisherman smiled, holding her gaze. 'My name is still William,' he said. 'William Riggs.'

'Rachel Castle. Nice to meet you again.'

They held each other's gaze for a little longer, then William looked down at the bag of fudge in Rachel's hand.

'I'm not great with too much sugar,' he said. 'Would you care to share it with me?'

'Uh … sure.'

'Great.' He pulled his hands out of his pockets, shook some water off his coat, and rubbed his hands together. 'I think if we stay out here this mist'll dissolve it, or at least turn it into sludge. Shall we go and sit somewhere indoors?'

Rachel felt a sudden prickling in her cheeks. There was literally nowhere she could go within a mile radius where someone she knew from school or her childhood didn't work. Rumours would have woven a spider web over the town by nightfall.

'Um, sure,' she muttered, giving half a shrug. 'How about the … ah, bus shelter over by the harbour?'

The last thing she had expected from William was a wide grin. Then, he doubled down by saying, 'Fantastic. My grandparents met in a bus shelter. Actually, it might have been a bomb shelter, but you know, the mists of time and all that.'

'The mists,' Rachel muttered, as William went to gather his things. While she watched him packing his belongings into a bag and folding up his deckchair, she wondered if he, or perhaps even both of them, was insane.

Sea mist cared not for gravity and the bus shelter seat was soaking wet, but rather than forcing her into the pub or a local café, William produced a plastic sheet for them to sit on, just large enough that they were able to leave a safety gap between them without either getting wet. Rachel used this free space to lay out the fudge, then held up the coffee and gave a shy smile, realising how the absence of a second might call her bluff.

'Ah … they'd run out of cups,' Rachel said. 'But if you have a cup, or perhaps some other container….'

William smiled and held up a flask. 'Sorted,' he said. 'Freshly ground this morning. Are you a coffee person?' He gave the flask a little shake. 'Guatemalan mountain blend,' he said. 'My favourite. Although, to be honest, it tastes just the same as the Kilimanjaro blend that was my favourite last week, or the Indonesian that was my favourite the week before. I've always liked the idea of being a coffee connoisseur, but after a certain price point, they all tend to taste the same.'

'Except for decaf, which always tastes rubbish.'

'That's the truest word I've heard spoken today.'

Rachel held up her cup. 'As far as I know, this is wholesaler mixed blend, but if you want, we can go halves on both and then do a taste comparison, just to settle it once and for all.'

'Sounds great.'

William unscrewed the flask lid and held it out. Rachel tipped up her cup, managing to get half of the coffee into the lid, while the other half dripped on the fudge waiting below.

'Ah, sh—'

'Coffee and cranberry,' William said. 'My favorite. Especially when the coffee half is hot.'

'I have a tissue somewhere….'

William stuck out a hand, briefly touching Rachel's hand as she moved to reach into her pocket. 'Don't worry.'

She looked up at him. 'Be happy, right?'

'No truer words.'

'So … how was the catch today?'

William looked down. 'Nothing biting.'

'That's too bad. Maybe tomorrow?'

William's mood abruptly changed. His smile dropped, a frown appearing in its place. Rachel tried to think of something else to say, but William stood up quickly as a bus's lights appeared through the mist, the vehicle lumbering down the street.

'I'm sorry,' he said. 'I didn't realise that was the time. This is my bus. Thanks for the fudge. I really appreciate it. See you around?'

'Ah … sure.'

And he was gone, grabbing his bag and running for the bus as it pulled in, the front door opening as it came to a stop. Through the fogged windows he was visible walking back and taking a seat on the opposite side, face turned away.

Something felt broken inside as the bus pulled away up the street, brake lights briefly flaring as it paused at a junction before heading up the hill and out of sight. Rachel stared after it for a few moments, then looked down at the untouched fudge lying on the plastic sheet William had lain down. He had left the sheet behind, but as Rachel scooped the fudge up, she noticed something lying on the ground below the seat, an oval made of black plastic.

She reached down and picked up the flask lid, its coffee spilt in haste on the gravel under the bench, and turned it over in her hands.

To her surprise, it had a name label taped along the outer rim—Graham Riggs.

He had said his name was William. Perhaps the flask belonged to his father, or a brother, but what kind of person put a name label on their flask? Rachel was tempted to go home and have a look online if her mother's wi-fi was working, but at the same time she felt so utterly deflated from William's sudden departure that before she knew what she was doing, she had turned and flung the lid into the river that ran along the inside edge of the harbour wall.

Almost immediately regretting it, she got up, winced at a sudden stab of pain in her foot, and stumped to the harbourside. The little cup was already out of range, bobbing around in the water a few metres offshore.

Wondering what it would feel like to be at the bottom of a collapsing stack of cards when every card was made of a sheet of steel, Rachel turned and hobbled slowly back up the road.

9

CELEBRATIONS AND ESCAPES

'Why don't you go down to the pub?' Linda said, as she stood in front of the mirror in the bathroom cabinet, the door open so she could talk to Rachel, who was sitting in an armchair in the living room, trying to get into an old, dog-eared thriller she had already read twice during her teens. 'You shouldn't stay in all the time. I can ask Colin to give you a lift, if you like.'

Rachel looked up. 'He's not just taking you to the pub, then?'

'What's that supposed to mean? If you must know, we're going to Brinton Manor, up in Portgate. You know, the one on the edge of Dartmoor? We used to go up there sometimes in the summer holidays.'

'We never went in it, just gazed longingly at it from a distance. Can Colin afford to take you in there on a fireman's pension?'

'There's no need to be like that.'

Rachel grimaced. 'Sorry. I'm just not feeling so good. I hope you have a nice time. Although, I can handle not being Cathy Ubbers' stepsister, if you know what I mean.'

Linda rolled her eyes, but from the way she gave a nervous shake of her head, Rachel could tell she had thought about it.

'I don't think we're quite at that stage yet. I imagine you're far more likely to get married than me. Go on, go down to the pub.'

'And choose a mate out of the fine selection likely on show?' Rachel gave up on her book and spread her arms. 'I'm damaged goods. Who would want me?'

Linda turned from the mirror and stared at Rachel, her smile dropping. She tilted her head and let out a little sigh.

'I would,' she said. 'I always would.'

'I assume you mean as a child, otherwise that's a bit creepy.'

Her mum chuckled and rolled her eyes. 'Of course I do. Honestly, you kids watch too many documentaries on YouTube these days. You're getting all these weird ideas in your heads.'

'Well, I would if the wi-fi worked.'

～

In the end, Colin Ubbers, driving a Mercedes that suggested a fireman's pension was really not so bad at all, dropped her off outside the Horse and Buoy Inn. She gave her mum a kiss goodbye and wished them a good evening, then stumped up the gravel path and through the pub's front door.

Years ago, the Horse and Buoy Inn had been a popular haunt. Over the years Rachel had gradually climbed the social maturity ladder from standing forlornly outside the beer garden fence hoping someone older would offer her a sly drink, to sitting at one of the coveted picnic tables while older kids sneaked drinks out to her, to standing proudly at the bar on a Friday or Saturday night, necking a few tequilas before heading off with whomever was that weekend's nominated driver to the clubs in Plymouth.

Good days. In her last couple of years at school, there had been a decent group of local kids and a few of the regular tourists, who'd hung out together over the summers. With the school year rolling around and the tourists dispersing, the winters had been long, but the weekends still fun and bright, when she'd hung out with Gavin and a few of their shared friends. Now, back in the village for the first extended period of time in several years, she felt nervous as she pushed through the door into the bar.

The old sights and smells remained, as perhaps they always had done. Alcove lights pushed the gloom back from the low ceiling into the corners. The same hanging vases of dried flowers hung from the walls, the same paintings of farming and fishing scenes that were too faded and poorly lit to see clearly, the same musty carpet smell mixed with that of real ale. Rachel imagined she could have stepped out of a time machine from 1850 and still felt at home in the surroundings.

It was only the people that had gone.

A well-to-do couple sat in a booth, finishing up a meal. An old man in Wellington boots sat on a bar stool, leaning over a pint. No one was behind the bar, but as she took a step forward a bell rang, and Simon, the young man who had been serving at Grandma Marigold's wake, appeared through a doorway into the connected family room bar.

Unable to escape, Rachel went up to the bar and pulled up a stool a couple down from the old man.

'Hey, Rachel,' Simon said. 'Pint?'

'Do I need to show I.D. this time?'

Simon shook his head, showing no sign that he

understood it as a joke. 'No, you're good. I checked you before.'

'Then I'll have a pint.' As Simon poured her a Carlsberg, the automatic response when no other brand was specified, Rachel leaned forward and said, 'Anyone likely to be in tonight?'

Simon chuckled and said, 'It's Wednesday,' as though that answered everything.

The old man, however, looked up. 'Floppy and Ben said they might stop by for a sly half.'

'You mean, Francis Jenkins and Benny Goodman?'

'Uh.'

'They're mates now?'

'Run Drifter's Hydraulics Repair and Maintenance up on Gillingham's Industrial Estate in Saltash,' the old man said.

'Really? They run a private business?'

'Doing well, tis.'

Rachel wanted to voice her surprise that two guys of her own tender age whom had never been friends at school could now be running a successful business together, but it was too tiring to find the words, so instead she took a long draw of the pint Simon had just set down.

'Ben's old man popped his clogs so Ben sold off his trawler rather than go into the family business,' the old man continued, seemingly happy for some company. 'You know what they're saying about cod stocks out in the Channel?'

Rachel had no idea, but she smiled and muttered something inaudible that the old man could take any way he chose.

'Old man would have turned in his grave, but he had a forklift so at least Ben's kept a bit of the old legacy. And Francis's old man flogged off a bit of land for that new waterworks up there so the boys went half n' half. That's the way, these days, ain't it? Ain't gonna know unless you take a punt. I'll tell you what, lads have bigger balls these days than we had as kids. Weren't no one gonna walk away from the farm for some big city lights and all that. So, you a local?'

Rachel felt sure she should recognise the old man, but he hadn't yet looked up from his drink. His voice, lime-scaled with age, sounded somehow familiar.

'I'm Rachel Castle,' she said. 'Linda's daughter, Marigold's granddaughter.'

'Huh.' The old man turned, and behind the whiskers and the lines and the liver spots there was something familiar about him.

'Al, you want a top up?' Simon said, leaning over to retrieve the old man's nearly empty glass, and in that moment Rachel remembered.

'Alan Marsh? Didn't you used to cut my grandmother's lawn?'

Alan's eyes gleamed. 'Built them flowerbeds down the bottom of her garden too,' he said. 'Fine, fine old lady.' He chuckled. 'Offered to replace your dearly departed grandfather once too, but she wasn't in the market.'

'I remember you. Didn't you have that old sheepdog? Reggie?'

Alan grinned. 'Archie. You and those kids from over the fence used to make such a fuss over the lad he'd come home of an evening and go straight to kip without dinner. Whoever heard of a dog like that?'

Rachel smiled as the mists cleared around her memories, and another thought came to mind. Alan had known her as a child, so perhaps he had known her—

The pub's door flew open, a sudden gust of wind making the hanging glasses over the bar rattle. Rachel turned to see Cathy Ubbers standing there, massively framed and massively pregnant, her blond hair billowing out behind her, one hand gripping each side of the doorframe as though the sea might suddenly rise up and try to reclaim her.

'Al, Si—oh, hi, Rach—call everyone you know. The party's on. O. M. G. I can't believe it. He finally asked me.'

'Lass, you getting a larger sty?' Alan said with a dry chuckle.

'Getting better than that, Al,' Cathy said, Alan's words going right over her head. 'We're getting married.'

10

EXPRESS DELIVERY

'You didn't have to stay so long,' Linda said, bringing Rachel another coffee and setting it down beside the plate of toast Rachel was yet to touch. 'You could have come home at any time.'

'Cathy literally barred the front door,' Rachel said. 'Once all her mates had shown up she dragged that old piano across so no one could get out, then ordered buckets of vodka and Redbull for everyone except herself.'

'Well, it's good to be responsible when you're pregnant.'

'She might not have been drinking alcohol, but she was slaughtering the karaoke from the top of the bar,' Rachel said. 'The craziest thing was that it was supposed to be an impromptu engagement party but Gavin wasn't even there. He was at home looking after Thomas.' Rachel sighed. 'I assumed they were already married. It was like getting punched in the stomach twice for the same reason.'

'No,' Linda said, sitting down opposite. 'They had one of these modern open relationships. I thought you knew.'

Rachel shook her head. 'I had no idea.'

'Are you going to the wedding?'

Rachel sighed. 'Cathy came up to me about eleven o'clock, put her hands on my cheeks and made me promise that I would come. I could see her contact lenses. She told me I needed to heal, and that she needed to know she was forgiven by having me attend my first love's marriage to someone else.'

'Oh, how unfortunate.'

'It was after that that I sneaked behind the bar and went out of a back door. I set off the burglar alarm, which kind of ruined the party for the rest of them, but don't tell anyone it was me if they ask.'

Linda patted Rachel's hand. 'Of course not.'

'How was your … date?'

Linda shrugged. 'Oh, it was okay. We might go out again, but I'm not sure. I don't know how many more anecdotes about burning buildings and cats stuck in trees or pipes I can take.'

'I'm sorry, Mum.'

'Don't be. We had fun. So … what are your plans for today?'

'I was going to stand in the river and wait for otters to burrow into my cast, freeing me from its grip at long last.'

'That sounds nice, almost poetic. If you have a bit of time beforehand, our washer's on the blink, so if you could take the laundry down to the launderette, I'd greatly appreciate it. I had to swap my shift last night for today's lunch shift to get the evening off.'

Rachel nodded. The laundry. The launderette. Where Cathy worked.

Surely, after last night, Cathy would have gone on some sudden pre-honeymoon, and be absent from work.

'Okay,' she said.

Her mother had a little wheelie cart which Grandma Marigold might once have used to haul shopping up the hill from the village. Rachel was able to balance the washing basket on top of it for the trip down the road to the launderette. It seemed like Porth Melynos had chosen this particular morning to have a spectator rehearsal for some upcoming event, because it felt like everyone Rachel had ever met was wandering about outside, greeting her with a kind smile before immediately glancing down at the trolley she was dragging along behind her. By the time she had reached the launderette, she was ready to climb into the washer with the clothes.

Her luck had finally taken a turn for the better, however, because an old woman Rachel didn't know was on duty, and Cathy was nowhere to be seen. After Rachel loaded the washer, she went back outside, but there was no distant wail of never-ending karaoke floating past her on the breeze. She imagined that by now Cathy was sleeping.

She went down to the harbour. A chilly breeze gusted through the streets and a few leaves fluttered past. The cliffs were slowly turning brown and orange, and Rachel took a deep breath, determined that today she would start over, bury all the disappointments of the past.

Near the breakwater she bumped into Francis Jenkins, who hadn't made it to the pub last night. Dressed in skintight Lycra running gear, sunglasses over his eyes and wireless headphones poking out of his ears, he shouted good morning to her just a little louder than was necessary, then ducked his head and charged for the hill leading up out of the valley.

One of the fishing boats was just leaving. Rachel briefly hoped that it was Gavin's, but was then glad to see it wasn't. Instead, she gave an anonymous wave to an unknown fisherman who sounded his horn in response while turning his boat out through the narrow channel towards the open sea.

As always, a few fishermen sat along the breakwater with their rods dangling over the edge, but there was no sign of William today. Rachel figured she might as well pass it off as one of those non-starters and forget about him, but she wasn't quite ready to let it go. There was the mystery of the missing fishing line, and the cup with another family member's name.

Like a mallet banging home the point, Rachel looked down and noticed something lying on the seaweed below the harbour wall, brought in by the last tide. The cup, the label still visible. She climbed down and quickly retrieved it.

Graham Riggs. William's brother, maybe? It was the kind of flask someone might take on a trip, so perhaps they'd got theirs mixed up somehow. Strange that it would be labeled, but perhaps they had two that looked the same. She stuffed it into her coat pocket, hoping she had the opportunity to return it to him sometime, then turned and headed back to the launderette, aware her washing would be done by now.

On her return, the old lady was nowhere to be found, but as Rachel took her clothes out of a washer and loaded them into an adjacent dryer, a door in the corner opened and Cathy Ubbers came bustling through, a washing basket under one arm, a box of single-use powder sachets under the other. At the sight of Rachel her eyes went wide, and she looked about ready to pass out.

'Rach….'

'Hi, Cathy.'

'Yesterday … thank you.'

Rachel pushed her last item into the washer and shut the door. She only had to get a pound coin into the slot and she could make an excuse to escape for twenty minutes.

'Seriously, thank you.'

Rachel grimaced, desperate to avoid the coming conversation. 'I had a ... good time.'

Cathy set the basket and the sachets box down, put her hands on the tables on either side and nodded.

'I know! Didn't you? And I thought it would be so awkward between us. But it's not, is it? We're like ... totally ... totally....'

Her face scrunched up, and she began to claw at the tables, long, purple-coloured fake nails scraping on the plastic.

'Cathy ... are you all right?'

'Oh ... my ... it's coming!'

It took a moment for Rachel to grasp what was going on. She felt the blood drain from her face as Cathy stared at her in alarm.

'The baby...!'

Cathy staggered. 'Quick, grab some towels!'

Rachel shook her head, barely able to bring herself to move. 'What...?'

'Number Three! Mrs. Wilmot ... she uses some posh ones. Quick, she'll be back in a minute ... get them on the floor.'

'All right, got it.'

Rachel jerked open the nearest washer door and pulled out a pile of warm, freshly dried towels. Her cast was making movement awkward, but she was able to lay them down on the ground and then help Cathy to half sit, half lie with her back against the nearest washer, the towels underneath her, her legs apart. In tight pink leggings covered by a pastel blue apron with STAFF emblazoned in black letters, she looked almost cartoon-worthy. As she puffed out her cheeks and exhaled in gasping, desperate breaths, Rachel wished she could step out of the TV and sit back and watch, instead of being forced to play a central part.

'The baby,' Cathy gasped, as though Rachel hadn't figured it out yet. 'The baby's coming!' Then, eyes suddenly flaring, she hollered, 'Turn the sign!'

'What sign?'

Cathy lifted an arm, a shaky finger pointing. 'That sign! I can't have Mrs. Wilmot coming in and seeing this … oh, we're breaking!'

'Where's the phone?' Rachel said. 'Cathy, where's the phone?'

'In the office. Don't leave me!' As Rachel tried to squeeze past, Cathy grabbed her arm, nails digging in. I can't do this alone!'

'Nor can I,' Rachel said. 'I have to call for an ambulance.'

'We wanted it natural,' Cathy sobbed, letting go of Rachel long enough for Rachel to slip past and hobble into the office, where a phone sat on a cluttered desk. 'We wanted it natural!'

'On the floor of a launderette isn't natural,' Rachel snapped, shaking fingers stabbing at phone buttons so scratched presumably from Cathy's fingernails that she couldn't read the numbers. If some company had decided to prank them and put the numbers in different positions, then she was lost.

'Rachel, quickly, it's coming!' Cathy wailed, as a voice on the phone line said, 'Emergency services. How may I be of assistance?'

'Rachel!'

'Is someone being murdered?'

'Not yet,' Rachel said. 'My … ah … friend is giving birth on the floor of the Porth Melynos Launderette. Please, please, please send an ambulance.'

'Have her waters broke?'

'Ah—'

'The tide's coming in and towels are getting wet!'

'I … ah think so.'

'Okay, well keep her comfortable, and if possible, try to time the contractions. We'll have someone over shortly.'

'Racheeeeelll!'

'Thanks, goodbye.'

Rachel put down the phone and hurried back into the other room, where Cathy was still lying spread-eagled and beached whale-like on the floor.

'Wa-wa-wa-water!'

'Ah … where? I can go across to the café—'

'No!' Cathy's eyes narrowed. 'This is just … just me and you.' Then, just as Rachel was starting to get triggers from her troubled playground days, Cathy's eyes widened and she began to puff out her cheeks with increasing regularity. Bright red, she resembled a bug-eyed goldfish.

'Is there some in the back room?'

'Tap!'

'Okay, got it.'

'Wait!'

Rachel turned back, making an awkward pirouette like a drunken ice-skater. She stuck out one hand to grab hold of the nearest table, felt its uneven leg wobble and nearly sent the whole thing crashing down on top of Cathy.

'Okay,' she said, getting control of both herself and the table. 'What?'

'My leggings,' Cathy gasped. 'Off.'

Please ambulance, come quickly, Rachel silently prayed as

she got down on her knees and began to tug at Cathy's leggings while the pregnant woman continued to puff and gasp. Leaning down, closer and closer to the critical area, she wondered what would happen if the baby decided to come right now. Would it just slide smoothly out like paper out of a fax machine, or would it come in a sudden rush? And if it came flying out, exploding into the world, would she be quick enough to catch it? Mrs. Grover had praised her dexterity skills at badminton club, but that had been a long time ago. She barely remembered how to catch a cold.

'No, no, no!' Cathy moaned as a tapping came from behind Rachel's shoulder. 'Get rid of her!'

Mrs. Wilmot was tapping on the glass of the closed door. The heat Cathy was giving off, coupled with a bit of autumn air, had managed to steam up the windows, and Mrs. Wilmot's finger worked in a circle, trying to clear the steam from the outside. Rachel ran over to the door and wiped a hand across the glass, causing the old woman to step back in alarm.

'I just came to pick up my towels. Is that Rachel Castle? I'm so sorry about your grandmother—'

'She's giving birth!' Rachel gasped, even as behind her, Cathy was shouting, 'Don't say anything! Tell her one of the washer's broke!'

'What? Oh my.'

'The ambulance is coming,' Rachel said, just as, to her relief, she saw it turn over the bridge further down the street and begin its way up past the tourist shops.

'Rachel! Quick!'

She turned back to Cathy, whose face had now gone beetroot red.

'It's coming! It's coming right now! Get over here!'

Rachel felt a sense of autopilot come over her. She

limped back to Cathy, stuck out her casted foot and lowered herself down, and suddenly her arms were filled with something slimy and wriggly, and Cathy was crying, gasping, panting, and over her shoulder someone was banging on the door and shouting, 'Excuse me, but could you please unlock the door?', and Rachel looked down, her eyes filled with tears, and then up at an exhausted but grinning Cathy, and said:

'I think it's a little girl.'

11

A SURPRISING ENCOUNTER

'It must be nice to finally be getting that cast off,' Linda said, as she steered her little car into the hospital car park. 'Although I imagine it'll be a little stiff for a while. Perhaps you should go swimming, or do some of that pool walking that's popular these days.'

'I was planning to run up the hill to Grandma's house every day,' Rachel said. 'Maybe take Francis Jenkins on in a couple of hill runs.'

'Oh, I wouldn't go that far. Well, here we are.'

Twenty minutes later, Rachel was sitting in a waiting room among a group of glum, frustrated people. Linda, reading a gardening magazine, was as chirpy as ever, but Rachel just wanted to get the process over with.

'We could go and see Cathy afterwards if you want,' Linda said. 'The maternity ward is just a couple of buildings over. I'm sure she'd be delighted to see you. After all, you did deliver her baby.'

Rachel grimaced. 'I was in the room when her baby was born,' Rachel said. 'I wouldn't say I delivered it.'

'Oh, she's been singing your praises from the rooftops,' Linda said. 'You're her new favourite person and all that. Melanie called me yesterday while you were at the café, just to say well done.'

'And to berate you for dating her ex-husband?'

Linda shrugged. 'We ended up having quite a bitch,' she said. 'Although you know, he called me again and suggested we go out again. I mean, perhaps I was a little harsh the first time....'

'Your life, Mum.'

'Rachel Castle? Room Three, please.'

'All right,' Rachel said, patting her mum on the knee. 'This is me. Wish me luck. Hopefully they won't chop my whole leg off with the cast.'

She got up and hobbled down the corridor on her crutches, hopefully for the last time. A nurse held a consultation room door open for her, and she went inside.

'Ms.... ah, Castle. Ah ... please take a seat.'

Rachel frowned at the uncertainty in the doctor's voice. She had been occupied in getting her crutches past a drip stand beside the door, but as the doctor turned in his chair, she realised why he had sounded a little strange.

William Riggs, the fisherman, now wearing a doctor's coat as he sat at a desk cluttered with files, pens and doctory ornaments like a plastic jigsaw model of a shoulder bone and the connecting tendons and a set of wind up false teeth, stared back at her. His cheeks had taken on a reddish tint, and she could sense him trying to maintain his professionalism. He made a show of typing something on his computer, then took a deep breath and turned back around.

'Hello again, Rachel.'

'Hi. Ah, William. I … ah … didn't know—'

'—that I was a doctor? I'm not, not really. I'm a locum doctor. I do all the minor stuff but don't have to make any of the big, scary decisions. Can you lift your foot up on to this chair, please, and I'll just check everything's in order.'

Rachel was finding it hard to speak without stuttering, so she just muttered, 'Thanks,' and did as she was told.

'I'm sorry about the other day,' William said. 'I didn't mean to look like I was rushing off or anything, but you know, there wasn't a bus for another two hours, and, well—'

His fingers were massaging her toes, tugging them, pushing them up and down. It wasn't an unpleasant feeling; Rachel thought she could get quite used to it if she had the chance. While she wanted to relax and let him do his work, at the same time she knew she had him cornered, and might not get another chance.

'I found your cup,' she said. 'You dropped it at the bus stop.'

'Oh. I wondered where that had got to.'

'I didn't bring it, but I have it at home.' She decided not to mention about throwing it in the river. 'Will you be going fishing down in Porth Melynos anytime soon?'

William shrugged. 'Probably. I'm only part time. Three days a week, usually. So maybe I'll see you down there on Thursday or Friday?'

'I'll keep an eye out for you.'

'Great.'

He had finished checking her. He opened a drawer and pulled out a pair of scissors. 'Your skin might look a bit strange, but don't worry,' he said. 'It'll be fine in a day or two.'

'Who's Graham?' Rachel asked.

William's hand jerked, and the scissor point jabbed into

her skin, leaving a tiny scratch. William muttered an apology as he scrambled for a piece of cotton wool.

'So sorry about that. I'll put a little cream on it and a plaster. I do apologise—'

'It's all right,' Rachel said, giving a dramatic wince. 'It's only a scratch. Not like the whole thing came off, is it?'

'I really am sorry. This will only take a minute.'

As he started to cut away the cast, Rachel took a deep breath. 'Why don't you have any fishing line on your rod?' she asked. 'I thought maybe you were taking a break or something, but when I saw you the second time, and then the third time, and you still didn't have any, I figured you weren't going down there to fish.'

As she spoke, William's cutting hand had paused. He didn't look up at her, but he uttered a little grunt and then continued cutting, pulling the cast away with his other hand. Rachel stared in dismay at the pearly white, wrinkled skin of her foot. And a moment later, the smell struck her, almost enough to make her gag.

'Is that … normal?'

'Your skin hasn't had any natural air or sun for a while,' William said. 'It'll be fine in a couple of days, though. I'll put a little cream on it and give you a prescription for some more. It'll be fine.'

He was changing the subject again, but in his persona as a doctor, he had a readymade excuse.

'It's okay if you don't want to talk about it,' Rachel said, staring at him until he looked up and met her eyes. 'But if you do, come and find me anytime. I'm working in the Sunset Harbour Coffee and Fudge Company, across the street from the launderette. I get the feeling you've had a little trauma in your life. I'm no expert, but my life isn't perfect. I recently both got made homeless and had a tree fall on my car. Although maybe it says that on your notes. About the tree, I mean.'

William looked up and met her eyes for a moment. 'Thank you,' he said, then quickly added, 'Ms. Castle, you're good to go. If you have any further problems, give reception a call.'

Rachel nodded, then stood up on her newly repaired leg and hobbled across the room. She glanced back as she reached the door, but William had his head down, and was typing something on the computer.

'Thanks,' she said.

If he heard, she didn't know. His head gave a slight incline, but he didn't look up. Rachel suppressed a sigh, then opened the door and went out.

12

GHOSTS OF PAST AND FUTURE

'You know,' Valerie was saying, leaning through the doorway out of the kitchen, 'A witch's magic works in mysterious ways. You could discover that your cast was the source of your power, and without it, you're nothing.'

Rachel lifted an eyebrow. 'Thanks?'

'You see, you managed to deliver a baby, and you met a boy—'

'I did not!'

Valerie gave her a frustratingly teacher-like look. 'You can't fool me. I spent forty years listening to pathetic lies. You met a boy, because you've been swooning ever since. Don't pretend you're not gazing lovingly out of the window because you're really interested in the rain or the car park over there. You're swooning.'

Rachel grimaced. 'I can't have this conversation with my mother, and all my friends seem to have disappeared, so it's kind of weird to have it with the science teacher who terrified me.'

'But you got good exam results, did you not?'

Rachel pouted. 'Yeah, pretty good.'

'You could have been a biologist. There's still time.'

'I'll think about it. I took journalism because—'

'Don't change the subject. We were discussing the boy.'

'Don't you have fudge to make?'

'It's October, it's a Wednesday, it's raining, and we haven't had a single customer all morning. Plus, I've read every single book on that rack. Some twice. So, no. I don't have fudge to make, nor anything else to do. Come on, cough up.'

Rachel sighed. 'Well, there's a guy I saw down on the breakwater. He was fishing without any line—'

'No one fishes without any line. That's a physical impossibility.'

'Well, he had a rod and stuff, but he was just holding it out over the water.'

'A spiritualist. Stay away. Those people are nuts.'

Rachel sighed. 'I don't think so. He had a flask with someone else's name on it. His brother or dad—'

'Which is not really suspicious at all, apart from having his name on it, which is a bit weird. I told you. Nuts.'

'I asked him, but he wouldn't tell me. And then when I went to get my cast cut off, he was the doctor.'

'Nice, unless you're into feminism and all that millennial hocus pocus. In which case, you'd better retrain. Not many journalists earn what a doctor earns.'

'I tried to ask him about it, but he wouldn't answer.'

'A mysterious type. Fantastic, until you find out he's a serial killer or one of those identity stealing fraudsters. Did he ask you for any money?'

'I had to pay a prescription for some cream.'

Valerie gave a curt nod. 'You're probably in the clear there. How old was he?'

Rachel shrugged. 'Between twenty-five and thirty-five,

I suppose. A little older than me, but not old enough that going out with him would be weird.'

'Promising. Now, the most important question. Was he good-looking?'

Rachel frowned. William wasn't the kind of person who'd be seen in any catalogues, or turn heads in the street, or have a large following of young women on social media waiting for him to post beachside pictures, but there was something about him … and the more she thought about it, the more she couldn't quite decide what it was. He had a nice smile. His eyes were gentle, and when he spoke, he had one of those voices that just made her feel calm, even if none of their meetings had been of that nature. She could imagine that in a comfortably lit room, with candles flickering, soft jazz playing, maybe a fire flickering in a hearth, she could have gone to sleep in his arms.

'That's a yes, then,' Valerie said.

'I didn't say anything!'

'You didn't have to. Now, we have to figure out how you can track him down. You have two options that I can see. You can take up pretend fishing, or you can injure yourself again.'

'Or there's option number three, which is to do nothing and forget about it.'

Valerie's eyes gleamed. 'Don't tell me you're about to give up on this?' she said. 'Don't you like a bit of a mystery? And isn't it a little exciting?'

Rachel grimaced. 'I don't know. Kind of, but you know, perhaps it's for the best. My family and men don't seem to go well together. My grandad died before I was born, and I have no memories of my own dad.'

'You don't?'

'He left when I was young. At least, I think he left. He

could be dead for all I know. My mother never talks about him.'

'Is that so? And you've never asked?'

Rachel shook her head. 'I've tried a couple of times, but she changes the subject or makes an excuse. She's not one to look back, is Mum. In fact, until Grandma died, I don't think I'd ever heard her talk about the past.'

Valerie gave a slow nod. 'Well, that's unfortunate. You have my sympathies. It appears you might still have a little healing to do, and how you do it is up to you. In the meantime, I do believe that at your age, making a few mistakes wouldn't hurt too much.'

'I don't want to—'

Valerie held up a hand and for a moment she was every bit the school teacher warding off an excuse.

'I know you think it's going to hurt, but in six months or a year you'll look back and wonder what all the fuss was about. Go on, dear. Dig a little deeper, push the boat out a little, as they might say around here. See what you can do and maybe even make yourself ha—'

The bell over the door tinkled as a man walked in. For a couple of seconds Rachel could do nothing but gawp as Gavin gave her a shy smile, lifted a hand in a half-wave, and then approached the counter.

'I'll let you deal with this one, dear,' Valerie said, then vanished into the kitchen and closed the door with a soft but authoritative thump.

'Rachel.'

'Gavin … ah … congratulations. On, ah, the baby, and your engagement.'

In a parallel universe someone might have been saying that to me. I walked away and left it behind, and here I am, right back where I started, without any of the good bits.

'Thanks.' Gavin closed his eyes a moment, then lifted a

finger as though about to impart a universal truth. 'I just wanted to say, thanks. For everything. Not just for, you know, delivering Raquel—'

'Raquel?'

Gavin's eyebrow rose. 'Oh, you didn't know? Cathy wanted to name her after you, but she thought Rachel was too … well, Raquel was more, you know, modern.'

Insulted and flattered in the same act. Cathy had a rare skill, and Rachel could only smile.

'Thanks … that's nice of her.' She gave an awkward chuckle. 'I think.'

'Cathy never stops praising you.'

'That makes a change.'

'She said you were like a rock, so calm under pressure, like a professional.' He gave the inside of the café a quick sweep with his eyes, a certain look of distain. 'Perhaps you should retrain as a midwife or something. You're wasted in here. Didn't you study newspapers or something?'

'Journalism,' Rachel said. *You know, Gavin. You were there when I chose my course and then you broke my heart when you said you wouldn't come with me.* A frog had caught in her throat, and was unseasonably trying to spawn or mate or something. 'I … studied journalism.'

'There's the parish council newsletter, but that's about it round here. Or were you thinking of going freelance?'

'I was thinking of leaving, but things haven't worked out like I planned,' Rachel said.

Gavin shrugged. 'You could write something about our boat if you like,' he said. 'Twenty-five years old next week is Bessie.'

'Bessie? It has a name?'

Gavin smiled. 'It's a nickname. Best Wind. Honestly, Dad would be happy to do an interview, provided he's done with the day's catch. Maybe you could publish it in *Fisherman's Weekly* or something?'

Rachel felt a scream building up inside her, and took hold of the edge of the counter, hoping to channel it, lightning-like, down through the floor instead of out into Gavin's face.

'I'll think about it,' she said. 'Was that why you came to see me?'

Gavin shook his head. 'No, no. I came to thank you, but also because Cathy and I wanted to ask you something. Obviously, Cathy can't be here, but—' He paused, looking down at his hands. *Maid of honour at their wedding. A live-in nanny.* It scared her to think that second wife in a polygamous relationship was actually her preferred of the options.

'We'd like you to be Raquel's godmother,' he said, looking up, a bashful smile on his face. 'It would mean a lot to us. Obviously, you wouldn't have to do much. Birthday and Christmas cards, and all that. It would just set our minds at ease to know that the person who brought little Raquel into the world would be there for her if something happened to us.'

The air seemed to dim. Rachel heard what sounded like the cawing of thousands of crows, their wings beating in a percussive rhythm. She wanted to raise her hands to shoo them off, but she was stuck rigid, her feet glued to the floor, her hands glued to the countertop. In front of her, through a browny-orange haze, Gavin—her first, and to date, only love—was smiling and saying something Rachel couldn't hear. The words droned like the bass keys on a piano held down together. Then, he was nodding, smiling, turning, leaving. Rachel stood still, waiting for herself to dissolve, as the door opened, and Gavin went out.

The tinkling of the bell was like an alarm pulling her back into reality.

She looked around to see Valerie standing beside her, and felt a bag of something being pushed into her hands.

'It's from the fresh batch. You need it. Go and sit down, and I'll bring you over a strong coffee. Double espresso, or do you really need me to sink the trawler and make it a triple?'

'Uh?'

'Triple it is. Give me a minute.'

Rachel slowly recovered the ability to speak. 'Did that ... really just happen?'

'Your ex-boyfriend—I'm guessing from your reaction?—just asked you to be the godmother for his child. Yes.'

'Oh. I had really hoped it was a dream.'

'I'm afraid not.'

'And ... ah ... what did I say?'

Valerie looked grave. 'You said yes. In fact, you said more than that. You said you'd be delighted.'

13

MYSTERIES UNEARTHED

RACHEL WAS LYING ON HER MOTHER'S SOFA, AND IT FELT like a good position to remain in until the end of time. Linda came in, whistling to herself, dressed in her work clothes with an unzipped coat over the top. She looked and sounded remarkably contented with her life. Her face wore a smile, and as their eyes met, Rachel felt a surge of love for the woman who had brought her up single-handedly for as long as she could remember. Sure, Grandma Marigold had been around, but it had been Linda who had wiped her eyes, picked the grit out of her knees, held her hair while she threw up, scrimped on her own clothes to buy new ones for Rachel, and a thousand other things.

'Have a good evening at work, Mum,' she said, forcing a smile that fought kicking and screaming not to come.

'Will you be all right? There's some Bolognese in the fridge.'

'I'll be fine. Will you eat at work?'

Linda grinned. 'It's carvery night. My favourite night of the week. I'll see if I can sneak you some leftover beef for some sandwiches tomorrow.'

She looked about to leave, but paused, looked and Rachel and cocked her head.

'Are you sure you're all right?'

Rachel shook her head. 'Life sucks.'

'Come on,' Linda said. 'There's a new episode of *Downton Abbey* on tonight. Or if you can't bear to stay in, there's a bingo night at the village hall.'

'I'll think about it.'

Linda lifted an eyebrow. 'Ah, I know what it is. The wi-fi.'

'Mum, I'm not that shallow.'

'I spoke to BT yesterday and someone will come round to look at it on Friday. If you're dying, though, I know the library is open until eight. They have computers you can use if you want to do your MySpace and all that.'

'MySpace....'

'Anyway, I'd better go. Are you all right to help me up at Grandma's tomorrow?'

'I start at two, so the morning's good.'

'Great. Try to survive until then. I have a feeling we're on the cusp of discovering her secret stash of diamonds. I'm absolutely certain they're inside that old cabinet in the cellar.'

'I'll try to hang in there,' Rachel said.

After Linda had gone, Rachel lay around a little more, but having got up late, it wasn't too likely she'd be able to sleep any time soon, and short of drinking more coffee or eating some leftover fudge she had brought from work, there wasn't any reason to stay in the flat. Television had never held much appeal, and she couldn't concentrate on a book.

Her newly minted foot always needed a bit of exercise, so she hauled herself up, put on a coat and went out for a walk. Instead of heading down to the harbour, she walked uphill, cutting through the large village car park which, outside the summer months, usually stood depressingly empty, to a shady forest path that followed the river for a mile or so before cutting up through the fields along old bridleways in the direction of Dartmoor.

The air was cool, biting at her skin. Leaves were starting to fall, piling up along the path for her to kick aside. Squirrels danced across the path, and she even spotted a rabbit up ahead before it darted into the woods. Alongside her, the river trickled and gurgled over the rocks, oblivious to the problems of the world as it made its gentle way down to the sea.

A couple of dog walkers greeted her, but otherwise, she was alone. It felt strange but nice at the same time, as though she was entering a period of restart. Autumn was the beginning of the end; soon winter would come, and then spring, and things could begin again.

But for now, she had to tie up loose ends. Gavin had left her heart damaged, but she was over him, or least close enough to move on. He belonged to Cathy now, and there was no turning back. It hurt, but she could deal with it.

Other such ghosts weren't quite so easy to bury.

It had been a while since she had felt the itch which had first taken her away from this village into the smoke, onto a university course she had hoped would lead her to greater things. She had once wanted to write, to investigate, to uncover and learn. Her utter failure to find a job in journalism had left her feeling jaded, and a succession of poorly paid temporary jobs that had made simply covering the rent the major stress of her life had done nothing to help. Now, as she felt herself able to breathe again, the urge to write was returning.

It was beginning to get gloomy under the trees, so she headed back into the village. The small library was not far from the car park, and when Rachel saw the lights on inside the windows, she couldn't resist. She went inside, spoke to a librarian who thankfully wasn't an old classmate, and logged on to a computer.

At first it was hard to get out of the old habits of checking social media and old favoured sites, but it seemed that little was going on in her old online world, and within a few minutes she had run out of things to check. For a moment she paused with her hands lifted over the keys and the cursor blinking in the search box, unsure what she wanted to type. Then, feeling a sudden rush of blood, she typed: 'William Riggs Graham Riggs'.

Searching for one or the other might have brought up social profiles or business pages, but linking them together meant any results would have to include both. Rachel wondered what to expect as the search icon circled, the library's wi-fi connection flickering from moderate to weak.

She stared as the results appeared. At first she couldn't be sure what she was seeing, then as her mind dealt with the sudden overload, she understood.

All of the articles on the front page dealt with the same event, and while the titles varied a little, they could all be summed up under the first, an article from the local paper dated September 17th, 2002.

Local man swept from cliffs
A coastguard operation has been called off this evening in the continuing search for local man Graham Thomas Riggs (44) of 14 Northcott Road, Saltash, who was swept from Smuggler's Point near Porth Melynos on the afternoon of September 16th. His son, William Philip Riggs (10), who was with him at the time and raised the alarm, was taken to safety and is recovering in a Plymouth hospital.

Rachel could only stare. The flask belonged to William's father. She knew Smuggler's Point; it was out along the coast path, a short way east of the harbour entrance. The cliffs there were treacherous, and part of the path had been fenced off for as long as she had known due to erosion and risk of collapse.

As a child, her mother had always warned her about being careful out on that section of coast path.

Now she knew why.

She searched a little further, looking for follow up articles.

Local man considered hero
Graham Riggs (44), of Saltash, was hailed as a hero today by Plymouth's city mayor after further details emerged concerning his disappearance. According to Rigg's son, William, the boy had got into difficulty when a section of the cliff began to collapse, plunging the boy into the water. Without thought for his own safety, Riggs entered the water and dragged his son to safety, before being swept away by what authorities are now calling a 'freak wave'. The mayor praised Riggs for his bravery.

Rachel searched further, but the articles became less frequent. Searches were called off, Graham Riggs' death was assumed, and a few months later he was awarded a medal for bravery in absentia. And there the trail ended.

Behind her, the librarian called to say the library would shortly be closing. Rachel pushed away from the computer and gave a slow nod.

She had some of the answers. William came down to the breakwater to be near to his father's memory, or perhaps he still had some dream that his father would return.

Rachel wiped a tear from her eye.

Outside, the wind had got up, and twilight had faded into night. The village's streetlights made a path along the single main street down to the harbour, then around the corner and up the hill, obscured by trees. On the hillside high above her, Grandma Marigold's house stood up there somewhere, hidden in the dark. Rachel looked up for a moment, a thousand memories flashing through her mind, then looked away, down towards the harbour, towards the line of terraced houses in which, halfway along and on the upper floor was her mother's tiny flat.

A flat in which Rachel had grown up. A flat disinfected of memories before a certain age, in which the narrative of Rachel's life that Linda required had been created, a little world in which she had always been happy, but from which her sense of mystery and wonder had been somehow filtered out.

As she listened to the autumn wind ruffling through the trees, sending flurries of leaves scattering across the deserted car park, the title of a yet-to-be-written newspaper article flashed into her head, and there it lodged itself, granite-like and immoveable, home to stay until she had satisfied its longing and her own.

A tale of two fathers.

14

INVESTIGATION

Poking through her mum's things felt like treachery, but Grandma Marigold's house was an open book. With her mother heading off to a Women's Institute coffee morning, Rachel offered to go up to Grandma's place and do a little more sorting in her absence.

The way in which Linda had undertaken sorting through Grandma Marigold's hoard of possible treasures (and a frightening amount of junk) told Rachel a lot about her own mother that she hadn't noticed before.

While most people might be drowning in nostalgia at the thought of sorting through a deceased parent's things, Linda had approached it with far greater practicality. The house itself had now been emptied of excess furniture; everything in poor condition had been taken to the local dump, and what was left was in a position to be either sold or retained as furnishings should Linda decide to rent the place out. All Grandma's bits and bobs, photos, mementoes and trinkets had been removed and carefully packed away for later consideration, stacked in boxes in the cellar. What Rachel might have considered her archives, however—the stacks of boxes and cupboards already in the cellar containing everything from faded packets of seeds to stashes of tatty and now out-of-use foreign currency—had been left mostly untouched.

After making herself a coffee, and donning a pair of plastic gloves—not at all in case her mother was checking for fingerprints, Rachel thought with a smile—she headed down into the cellar.

While Grandma Marigold hadn't been a hoarder to the degree that people on reality TV shows could be, she had still saved an awful lot of stuff. Rachel found herself picking through bags of collectible tokens from cereal packets, boxes of assorted individual socks, packs of unopened commemorative stamps, crates filled with miniature ceramic houses, and all manner of other bits and bobs. Aware that her mother would likely eventually get to it, she put everything gently aside, looking for the real treasure buried beneath.

Finally, after shifting aside a pair of old curtains that were blue around the edges and grey where the sun had caught, she found what she was after.

Photo albums.

There had been some around the house, of course, the ones that Grandma Marigold had pulled out from a drawer at the bottom of the old bureau, lifted a young Rachel up onto the sofa beside her, then opened the large, leather-bound books over both their knees. They had smelled of dust and stuffy, unopened rooms, felt rough under her child's fingers like how she imagined alligator skin might feel.

Together they had looked at the sepia pictures of long-dead great-aunts and uncles, moving slowly forward through time to the obligatory photograph of Linda in hospital with a newborn baby in her arms, the baby that within a page of oddly bland landscapes of the moors and the cliffs had become a bathing infant, then a child on a tricycle, and finally a little girl smiling sweetly into the camera, a gleaming school uniform still with ironed creases along the arms.

Rachel remembered those days with great fondness, those memories that always seemed to happen at this time of year, when the weather was cool and the wind was hassling the trees and leaves were piled up on the paths. Now, though, as she thought of it, all she'd ever seen, and what those albums had contained was the sanitised version of her life, that placed on show, the narrative as her grandmother and mother wanted it.

Now she was looking for the outtakes.

The first box she came across contained smaller albums, the kind given away for free by printing shops, and here Rachel found pictures she had never seen before but looked familiar regardless, the less aesthetic versions of the ones that had made the final, on-display cut, multiple pictures of herself on a tricycle from different angles, her head turned partly away, one arm out of shot, a smear of over exposure on one side. There was Grandma Marigold, leaning over a car, a crack of bottom showing above slipped jeans in a comical version of the one that had made it into the album. Rachel smiled, but it wasn't what she was after. Moving the box aside, she dug deeper, looking for more.

After another half an hour, she stopped for more coffee, going upstairs and sitting by the table that gave her a view down over the village. Yet to uncover what she wanted, she had nevertheless come across pictures of her mother as a young woman, permed hair, hideous eighties fashion, aping dance poses that would have made John Travolta burn his shoes in shame.

Yet that elusive clue she was after eluded her: a picture of her father.

Linda Castle had lived a life of forward motion, forever looking to the future, to tomorrow, to what was on the horizon. There were no sunsets in her life, only sunrises, new days, new challenges. There was no reason to regret anything, because what was done was done and wasn't worth crying over. Rachel had never wondered much about her father because there had been no need to wonder; he was in the past and the past was done. The future was the only thing that mattered.

The official narrative, brief though it was, was that her father had left them when Rachel was young, no more than three or four years of age. She had a vague memory of a man being around, but sparingly, as though he had popped in from time to time but never been a part of her life. She had no name for him, no face, and had never had much longing. Looking back, she had often wondered if her memories of this supposed father had actually been of the postman, or milkman, or perhaps a friendly neighbour.

By the time she was old enough to have solid, visual memories, this supposed father figure was long gone.

She went through another box, and found nothing. In another, at the very bottom of the pile, she found a cache of baby photos. Sure at last that she had found what she was looking for, she went through them in earnest, certain that here she would finally find what she was looking for.

Instead, all she found was innumerable outtakes of those which had made the final album cut. Not a picture of a man in sight, not even a man's arm, or leg, or other body part getting a quick poke into the side of a picture.

Wondering if she was perhaps the Second Coming but no one had let her know—although it was possible Cathy

Ubbers believed so—she retreated to the living room for more coffee.

She was getting nowhere. Grandma Marigold's supposed treasure trove of memories had uncovered plenty of nostalgia, but was keeping its cards close to its chest. If there were secrets somewhere, they weren't revealing themselves. Rachel had hoped to uncover some Pandora's Box of revelations, but although she'd found a bag of grimy old keys, every single one was labeled with such thrilling titles as 'blue suitcase', 'cellar door spare' and 'upstairs bedroom window (old)'.

As she sat by the window with her hand cupped around a coffee mug, she gazed down into the harbour, wondering if one of those men she interacted with daily could actually be her father. What if it was Mr. Wilmot, owner of the local fish'n'chips shop, or Alan Marsh, her grandmother's gardener? What if—god forbid—it had been one of her friend's dads, one who'd perhaps met her mother in a moment of vulnerability and taken advantage? What if—worst case scenario—it was Colin Ubbers, and she was actually Cathy's half-sister? She'd never noticed any genetic resemblance between herself and her former nemesis turned happiness tormentor, but her mother and Melanie Ubbers were as different as cats and dogs so might be hiding whatever genetic similarities Colin Ubbers was providing. What if her mum ended up married to Colin, and he became not only Rachel's step-dad but her actual dad at the same time?

She leaned forward, wondering if she could squeeze her head into the coffee mug and drown. It was unlikely, but if she pressed hard enough....

She looked up again, squinting out through the window at the village below. It had started to rain, draping the village with a grey veil. And there, down on the breakwater, as other fishermen began to pack away and leave, she saw a familiar figure.

William was back.

He probably wanted to be left alone. But even if he did, at least—thanks to William, of course—Rachel now had two working feet on which to pursue him.

Rachel finished the coffee, gave the cup a quick rinse under the tap, then headed for the door.

15

ON THE HOOK AND OFF AGAIN

It was bucketing down by the time she reached the harbour and walked out along the breakwater. She had borrowed an old raincoat hanging on a rack inside her grandmother's front door, and found an umbrella inside a cupboard, but it was that slowly falling type of heavy rain, which seemed to soak her regardless. Grandma had had the daintiest of feet, so her Wellington boots had been too tight a squeeze for Rachel, and now her trainers were soaked, water squishing between her toes as she walked out to where William sat huddled on his deckchair.

'Hello,' she called over the relentless patter of the rain and the crash of the swell on the breakwater wall as curtains of spray splashed across her. 'I just came down here to say thanks again for getting me out of that horrible cast.'

William looked up. In the shadows beneath the hood of his coat, his expression was unreadable. 'You're welcome,' he said.

Rachel took a step closer, wincing as her foot slipped into a pothole, cold water sloshing over her ankle.

'I was wondering if I could talk to you about something,' she said.

William shrugged. He shifted the rod on his knees, revealing that once more no line hung through its hoops. If he said anything, it was lost beneath the sound of the rain.

Rachel hooked a thumb back over her shoulder, grimacing as a dribble of water ran up her forearm, soaking one of her few previously dry places.

'You see that café over there? I pre-ordered two pasties, two scones, and two large coffees. You don't have to come, but as a doctor, you'll have to deal with the guilt of my cholesterol level for the rest of your life if you don't. If you do come, you at least can save me a little by eating half, and perhaps even a bit of my pasty's crust, because I usually struggle with it. What do you say?'

For a moment William just stared at her. Then, from under the hood Rachel caught a glimpse of a small smile.

'Sure,' he said.

∽

A couple of borrowed towels could work wonders, and twenty minutes later, Rachel sat in a window seat, facing William across a pretty white-washed table while the rain battered down outside.

'How was today's catch?' Rachel said, as a waitress set down two coffees and went back into the kitchen.

William shrugged, but the hint of a smile played on his lips. 'Nothing really biting,' he said. 'How's the foot?'

Rachel wiggled her toes, covered only by a hand towel the waitress had lent her. 'It moves again. Thanks.'

'All in a day's work. So … you live around here?'

Rachel nodded. 'I keep trying to escape, but it's not working very well. And you're not from round here?'

'Actually, my dad was. He grew up here, and always loved it, so Mum said.'

'Your dad … he … died here, too, didn't he?'

William looked down. Rachel reached out a hand, pulling it back before she put it over his.

'I'm sorry, I didn't mean to be nosy.' She frowned, then shook her head. 'Actually, I did. You see, before my life got derailed by lots of stupid stuff like unemployment, broken bones, and homelessness, I studied to be a journalist.'

William looked up. 'Did you now? Then maybe you can tell me what happened?'

Rachel felt a little uncomfortable at the accusatory look in his eyes, but supposed that in a way she deserved it. After all, she had hounded him. He had only wanted to be left alone.

'I brought your flask lid,' Rachel said, reaching into the kangaroo pocket of the almost-dry hoodie she wore and pulling the little plastic cup out. 'The one I told you I'd found?'

As she passed it across to William, his eyes lit up.

'I appreciate it,' he said. 'Actually, I stopped by your café a couple of days ago, but you weren't there.'

Rachel stared. 'Really? No one said.'

'I didn't say anything. I just had a look at some trinkets and bought some fudge. They probably thought I was a tourist.'

He looked away, out of the window at the rain-drenched harbour hiding behind the mottle of raindrops battering the glass.

'I'm sorry, but I looked you up.'

William looked back at her. 'What did you find?'

'I read about your dad. I'm really sorry. That's why you come down here, isn't it?'

William frowned, and for a moment Rachel wondered

if he would cry. She didn't know what she would do if he did; there were no tissues on the table and the only towel she had at her disposal was currently draped over her bare feet.

'He used to take me fishing out on the cliffs,' William said. 'He loved fishing. His job was so demanding, but he always found time to take me out on the weekends. It was our special time together. I loved those days.'

'He sounds like a kind man,' Rachel said.

William smiled. 'He was my hero,' he said. 'I idolised him. I think my Mum was jealous, but I used to wait at the door for him to get home, and our weekends together, they were just perfect. We'd go out on the cliffs, find some secretive little spot, and then throw our lines out into the water. Sometimes we'd catch something, sometimes not. But we always had fun. Dad would ask me about what I wanted to be in the future, and tell me about far off places he'd visited. I'd tell him things I'd never told my friends or even Mum, sometimes just stupid things, about school, or what I was feeling, and he'd never ever laugh, or mock me, or belittle me, even though I was just a kid. He treated me like an adult long before I ever became one, and made me feel like the most important person in the world. He was a wonderful dad. And then, he … he was gone.'

William's hands had clenched over the edge of the table, and he leaned over, looking down. The waitress appeared again and set down their pasties, but William didn't look up. He continued to stare at the tabletop, his shoulders trembling silently as he dealt with a level of grief Rachel had never known. All she could do was stare, and then finally pluck up the courage to pat him lightly on the back.

'I'm so sorry,' she said.

At last William took a deep breath and looked up. His

eyes were red, but he swiped away his tears with a quick brush of his hand.

'It was a long time ago,' he said. 'I ought to be over it by now. It's never really left me, you know?'

Rachel nodded. 'I can't imagine what it must have been like. To lose your father like that. I mean– –'

Williams eyes narrowed. 'Are you doing your reporter thing on me?'

Rachel gave a frantic shake of her head, but her eyes must have given her away. 'I'm sorry, I didn't mean to intrude. I just wanted—'

'Thanks for the coffee,' William said, standing up and swiping his coat off the back of the chair so quickly it sprayed Rachel with droplets of rain. 'I'll see you around.'

He picked up his bag and was gone, marching across the empty café and out through the door before she could even think to follow. As she scrambled up to give chase, she watched him through the rain-smeared windows as he marched along the harbourside, back towards the shops and the bus stop. He was already out of sight before she remembered she was still barefoot.

With a sigh she sat back down, just as the waitress reappeared from the kitchen.

'Would you like your scones with your pasties or after?' she asked, giving Rachel a sweet smile.

'Ah ... actually, can I just have them for takeaway?'

'Sure.'

'And can I also take away one of these pasties? I'm afraid my friend had to ... leave early.'

'No problem.'

Rachel sat back in the chair and let out a deep breath. If fishing was easy, she was certainly doing a poor job of hooking William. She had thought she had got him for a while, but now she just felt awful. Perhaps he was right, and she was being too intrusive, or doing it for her own selfish gains. She had hoped to maybe help him, because someone who sat at the end of a breakwater in the pouring rain while pretending to fish clearly needed a bit of a leg up.

She realised the waitress was still standing over her table.

'Don't worry, dear,' she said with a kind smile, as though witnessing breakups was a daily event. 'If you eat your pasty, you'll feel much better. Trust me.'

16

A SET OF NEW CARPETS

'You should smile more,' Valerie said, standing in the doorway to the kitchen with a tray of freshly baked fudge in her hands. 'Otherwise, I feel like I'm looking into a mirror at a younger version of myself.' When Rachel just gaped, Valerie lifted an eyebrow. 'Oh, you might be under the assumption that I wasn't as pretty as you, but I can assure you, that was an act to keep you unruly schoolyard scum in your place. Of a Saturday night down Plymouth with a bit of paint on the face and my hair up, I was quite the honeypot. I snared many an unsuspecting sailor.'

Rachel just stared. 'That's ... great.'

'Even got one to marry me,' Valerie said. 'But ... he died. I didn't kill him, if that's what you think.' She smirked and gave Rachel a wink. 'I made him suffer first.'

Unsure to what extent she ought to believe her former teacher, Rachel just bobbed her head and forced a smile.

'Ah ... is this better?'

'Beautiful. So nice, in fact, that I think this fudge is melting. Better get it into the display case quick sharp.'

'I didn't think fudge could melt?'

'It depends on the beauty of the person selling it. Now, what's happened to you?'

Rachel wasn't sure where to start, so she figured she'd just pick a random point and jab a stick into it in the hope of striking gold.

'I don't suppose you remember my father?'

'Your father? I'm afraid I've not been living here that long. Didn't he die?'

'I don't actually know.'

'Well, perhaps you need to ask your mother.'

Rachel winced. 'I'm scared to try. She's never really spoken about it, and never made it a big deal, so I've never really wanted to know.'

'Everyone wants to know who their father is. Can't you have a look at your birth certificate?'

'I did. Only my mother is listed. Under father, it just says 'unknown.' That can't be right, though, because I have a vague memory of him. I'm sure he was there until I was three or four. Or at least, someone was. I don't really know.'

'It really sounds like you need to have a conversation with your mum. Do you want some rope in case you need to tie her up? There's some around the back. Clara had this worry about the sign out front in the winter storms, but I can let you have it for a day or two.'

Rachel shook her head. 'No, but I might need to lock her inside. If I ever even mention it, she pulls an immediate runner.'

'She probably doesn't like to talk about it. It's rare that any relationship ended happily, not to mention the guilt she must feel that you grew up without a father. I'm sure it's a very sensitive subject, but at the end of the day, it's information that's owed to you, no matter what she says.'

Rachel nodded. 'I suppose I'll just have to try. I think

all I really want to know is his name. And, well, who he was, and—'

'So basically everything.'

Rachel gave a sheepish nod. 'I suppose.'

'Well, good luck with it. And if you need a shoulder to cry on, Clara will certainly be willing. I, of course, will be a little more reluctant, but you're shop-family now, and we're both there for you.'

Rachel had almost forgot she was talking to her old secondary school science teacher, and felt more like Valerie was a stern old aunt. She smiled.

'Thanks.'

'Good luck.'

~

'Mum … can I have a word?'

Linda was stirring tea in the kitchen with a musical clinking of the spoon on the cup. She turned as Rachel came in and smiled.

'Sure. What about?'

Rachel steeled herself. She opened her mouth but words didn't come out.

'Are you all right?'

'I—'

'Would you like a cup of tea?'

'No, I—'

'Or a biscuit? I might have to nip to the shops—'

'Dad!'

Linda flinched back. 'Excuse me?'

Her mother was already stepping back out of range, so Rachel took a step forward and put a hand on her mum's arm.

'I want to know about Dad. Please, Mum.'

Linda gave a strange shudder, as though trying to throw the feeling off. She started to twist in the direction of the door, but Rachel kept hold of her arm and was dragged along behind her.

'Mum, please, I don't want to upset you. I just want to know. I don't even know his name.'

Linda, perhaps realising Rachel wasn't going to let go, relaxed. She lowered her arms to her sides and took a deep breath.

'Okay, if you really want to know … I'll need my cup of tea, and you'd better make one for yourself. Can you bring them over to the table?'

Rachel, suddenly tingling with excitement, nodded. 'Sure. Just stay right here.'

She hurried back into the kitchen, where the tea Linda had been making sat on the counter next to the kettle. She made one for herself, her fingers shaking, barely able to hold the spoon. *She's going to tell me. At long last, she's going to tell me. After all these years….*

The thud of a door closing in the other room was like a hammer banging a stake into Rachel's heart.

She's fooled me again. She's done a runner.

Ignoring the tea, Rachel went back into the living room, only to find it empty. Her shoulders dropped. In her eagerness to believe Linda, her mother had bolted.

Perhaps now she would never know.

She was just turning back to the kitchen, wondering if there was something stronger she could drop into the tea, when the master bedroom door opened and Linda appeared, holding something tiny in her hands.

She looked up at Rachel and smiled. 'Did you get the tea?'

'Mum … I thought … you….'

Linda shook her head. 'I suppose it's time you knew. Here.'

She held out the little card. It still looked new, the corners square and sharp. A business card. Rachel took it and turned it over in her fingers.

Chad Evans
Carpeting and Upholstery
14 Fore Street, Brentwell
Tel ---
'You'll N-evans find a better carpet!'

Rachel looked up. 'Is this some kind of a joke?'

Linda shook her head. 'No. That's him. That's your father.'

'My father's name is Chad?'

Linda shrugged. 'And I think it was Charles or something. He fitted your grandmother's carpets. She was getting old, and I was still living at home at the time, so I … took charge.'

'I bet you did.'

'Rachel, don't judge me.'

'I'm sorry, I didn't mean it like that. I'm just struggling with this. And … this is the worst pun ever.'

'He had a way with jokes,' Linda said. 'We went out for fish'n'chips once, and he was all like 'This is a great plaice' and 'Have you haddock enough? I don't trout this is the best fish shop in town'.'

'Ouch.'

Linda shrugged. 'You can see why the relationship didn't last.'

'But I remember him. I mean, not really, but there was a man there. I remember him picking me up.'

'I … met him when he did the living room carpet.'

Linda shook her head. 'And a year or so later we replaced the carpet in the hall. Then, a while after that, the one in the bathroom. He also did kitchens, so we had him do the lino in there. You must have been about four by then. He was a friendly enough guy, always picked you up and gave you a bit of a tickle. You seemed to get on very well.'

'And he didn't know?'

Linda took hold of the sofa's armrest and lowered herself down. Rachel sat down beside her.

'I told him when you were about four. We'd just had that little bit of carpet just inside Grandma's front door changed. I'd had the flu for a week or so, and I suppose I was feeling vulnerable.'

'What did he say?'

Linda sniffed. A single tear ran down her cheek. 'He seemed really happy. He scolded me for not telling him, then picked you up, and spent the next hour or so playing with you.'

'Didn't Grandma think that was a bit weird?'

'Oh, no, she'd gone off to one of her stitch and bitch sessions at the village hall. Life goes on, doesn't it?'

'He played with me?'

'Yes. He was quite upset that I hadn't told him, and I was quite upset too. After all, it had only been a once off, you know, and I was never quite sure how to bridge the subject. I felt so foolish, but even though whatever attraction there had been between us had long since died, I thought maybe he'd be part of your life.'

'So what happened?'

'He promised to get back in touch, but he never did. And the next time I tried the number on the card, it had changed.'

'Didn't you try to look him up?'

'Well, I always planned to. I mean, I kept putting it off

and putting it off, and before I knew it, a couple of years had gone by. We didn't need any more carpets—he did a really good job, and they were decent quality, you know—and this was in the days before everything was online. Not long before, but long enough. And I was never much into computers, and after a few years, I just sort of gave up. I figured he wasn't interested, and that was it, really.'

A window was slightly ajar, letting in a cool autumn breeze. The sky was clear, the sun bright overhead. Rachel stared at her mother, unable to bring herself to speak.

'I know I should have told you,' Linda said, shaking her head. 'But I didn't like to look back, you know? I tried to be the best mother I could be and hoped that would be enough.'

'I know.' Rachel went over to the sofa and put her arms around her mother. 'You were, Mum. I love you so much.'

Both of them were crying. Outside, a seagull gave a jarring squawk, and a pot of dried flowers just inside the window rustled as the wind gusted. Rachel held on to her mother, glad beyond words that her mother hadn't gone the way of her father, yet at the same time feeling an urge in her bones to know more.

Who was Chad Evans? And why had he never come back?

17

ON THE CLIFFS

'You seem a little quiet today,' Valerie remarked, as Rachel handed a bag of fudge to a customer, then forced a smile and muttered a brief thanks. 'You've barely said a word all morning.'

'Sorry,' Rachel muttered. 'I'm feeling a little under the weather.'

The doorbell tinkled and Clara walked in, holding up two shopping bags, one with Tesco on it, and another with H&M.

'Back from the big smoke,' she said in a cheery singsong voice. 'You wouldn't believe how much I spent in actual, real life shops. At least fifty pounds. I feel like the world is wobbling on its axis.'

'How was the festival?' Valerie asked.

Clara clapped her hands together, the bags colliding with a soft thud. 'Oh, it was fantastic. So lovely to see my old pupils, but I wouldn't go back for a second. Their new teacher seemed to be just about coping, but it was infinitely preferable to be an observer rather than in charge. How are we all here?'

Valerie gave Rachel a pointed look. 'The youngster has family and relationship issues,' she said. 'I believe we need to stage an intervention.'

'I'm not—'

'Fudge always helps, dear,' Clara said. 'Fudge and coffee. The lethal combination.'

'The issue seems to be Breakwater Boy,' Valerie said.

'What?'

'The Phantom Fisherman,' Clara added. 'We've discussed him at length over the phone.'

'You—'

'Both of us believe you should let it go,' Clara said. 'He'll come back when he's ready. I mean, just look at you. You're a delight. He'd be a fool not to.'

'Or gay,' Valerie added.

'Well, there is that. But we'll give him the benefit of the doubt for now.'

Rachel's cheeks were burning. 'I appreciate your interest in my love life, but things are … complicated.'

Valerie and Clara crowded around. 'Well, dear,' Clara said. 'A problem shared is a problem halved, or in our case, a problem thirded. Is that a word?'

'You ought to know,' Valerie said. 'Writing all your teacher plays and all that.'

'It's not a commonly used word,' Clara said. 'But it will do. In any case, let's just sit down and have a chat. It's not like we're busy, is it?'

At that exact moment the door opened with a tinkle of the bell and a swoosh of the wind, and like a witch returning from the moor Cathy Ubbers marched in, a tiny bundle held in her arms.

'I just got home from hospital,' she said. 'The doctors told me to rest, but I just couldn't keep my feet still. I just had to show off this little one. Val, Clar—' She turned and winked at Rachel, '—and *Godmother* Rach, meet baby Raquel.'

She pulled back the blanket to reveal a shriveled little thing that looked to Rachel like a giant baked bean with a face and arms. The two old ladies immediately descended into a chaos of coos and aahs, and when the baby opened its mouth a little the feverish response rose another pitch. Rachel just stared, her eyes glazing over, thinking of another path she might have trodden.

'Isn't she so adorable?' Cathy was cooing. 'And doesn't she look so much like Gavin? She's going to be a heartbreaker for sure.'

Rachel couldn't handle any more. She turned away, stepped back behind the counter, and began to shovel lumps of fudge into her mouth.

∼

Luckily her miniature breakdown had happened at the end of her shift, and she was able to make it as far as the harbour before being sick in the river. Then, feeling the need for both fresh air and some exercise to offset that fudge which had got into her system, she decided to take a walk out along the cliffs on the eastern side of the harbour.

It had been years since she had come out this way. Always there, the steep ups and downs of the coast path had for most of her life been something she would do *tomorrow*, and barring a couple of school trips and one or two brave teenage expeditions, she had never really spent much time out on the rocky, treacherous headlands that sheltered the village from whatever winter rage the English Channel could muster.

However, as she struggled up steep, rocky paths with the wind trying to rip her jacket from her shoulders, then dropped down deep ravines revealing tiny, hidden inlets, she began to understand the appeal. The scenery was wild but beautiful, rugged yet picturesque. From the tallest part of the headland she could see the coast stretching away both east and west, windswept cliffs pitching straight into the water, towns and villages nestled in the hollows in between.

The section of the path that had once led to Smuggler's Point was still cordoned off by a frayed red rope hooked through leaning metal stakes. She straightened a couple, pushed back in a couple more that had worked loose, then looked down the old section of path towards the narrow strip of headland that hung out over the water, just a couple of metres above the sea.

She knew nothing about fishing, but from an objective point of view, it looked like a good spot. The water was deep there, and the inlet channels on either side would provide shelter to fish. She could also see where the cliff appeared to have collapsed, though, soil and rocks exposed by slippage.

Was this where Graham Riggs had met his end?

What would a journalist do? Would they climb down there, take some pictures, get a feel for the place, try to reimagine what had happened?

Rachel stared down the grassy slope at the pointed headland. Where rock had fallen away, the exposed surface had begun to vegetate over, and in calm seas it wouldn't have been so dangerous, being just a couple of metres above the water's surface at its lowest point.

Today, the water was choppy but lacked the power of a winter storm. Rachel paused for a moment, then stepped over the protective fence and started down the old path. It led through the grass towards a flat, narrow point. The tide was low, a few rocks exposed at the headland's base.

Rachel reached the narrow promontory and paused. Around the neck the rock had eroded, falling into the sea, before it widened out a little. On a flat rock in the centre, stood a pyramid of piled stones. In front, a flat piece of slate stuck out of a gouged crack in the soil.

Something was written on it. Rachel took a step forward to get a better look, and her foot twisted, a rock coming loose under her shoe. Pain raced up from her bad foot, and she slipped as the path crumbled beneath her feet.

'Watch out!'

Water sloshed over the rocks below, and Rachel braced herself for a wet, painful fall, only for a hand to close over her arm and haul her back. She sat down heavily on a bed of thick, springy grass as a shadow fell over her.

'What on earth were you playing at?' William snapped, hands on hips like an angry teacher. 'There's a reason this section is fenced off.'

'I'm sorry … I just wanted a look.'

'Well, don't. It's dangerous down here. The ground is unstable.'

Rachel met his gaze. 'You're down here.'

'That's because I was following you.'

'Why were you following me? And you must have been pretty sneaky about it. I didn't see you.'

It was William's turn to look embarrassed. 'I … I … was … making sure you didn't do anything stupid.'

'It's a good job you did, then, isn't it?'

William's shoulders relaxed and he sighed. Giving a resigned shake of his head, he sat down on the grass beside Rachel.

'This is where my father disappeared,' he said.

'I know. I looked it up. Before you have some big tantrum and run off again, though, I wasn't spying on you, or planning to sell some sneaky article to the tabloids. I was just interested. I was interested in … you.'

William stared out to sea, not appearing to have heard her. For a long time he said nothing, and as she waited, Rachel felt her own rush of anger slowly filtering away, down through the earth and out into the sea. She closed her eyes for a moment, then heard William sigh.

'It's so beautiful along here,' he said. 'Especially in this season, when the wind has a chill about it and the sea is getting choppy and wild. We used to come fishing down here, just me and Dad.'

Rachel said nothing. If William was ever going to open up about himself, it was now. She followed his gaze out to sea, tracking the line of a passing ship on the horizon.

'We were down here that day. Sat on the end of that point, blankets over our knees. The wind was getting up, and the sea was getting rougher, and Dad said it was time to call it a day. We started to pack up our stuff, but as I turned to my bag, my rod slipped. It was halfway down, on the shale bit right there, just above the water. I was a kid, I didn't think. I reached for it, and slipped.'

He fell quiet again, and Rachel risked a glance at his face. Tears had filled his eyes, and as she watched, one beaded and trickled down his cheek. His chest had started to rise and fall with barely controlled sobs.

'I went into the water, headfirst. I hit some rocks and badly bruised my chest and legs, but before the waves could get to me, Dad came in after me. He grabbed me, held me up and pushed me until I could get hold of something. Just as I pulled myself up on to the grass, a swell came in.' He paused, openly crying now. 'I didn't even see him go. I turned around, and he was gone.'

Rachel reached out and pulled William into her

shoulder. He cried for several minutes before finally wiping his eyes with his hand.

'I'm sorry,' he said. 'It's hard to talk about. After it happened, I ran back to Porth Melynos, into the nearest shop and asked for help. They had helicopters out and everything, but they never found him. I had to explain it over and over again, to the coastguard, police, my mother … but it was always about the facts. What happened? How did it happen? Where exactly did he go into the water? How high was the wave?' He flapped his hands and shook his head. 'It was always about facts. It was never about how I felt, what I saw in his eyes that day, how it felt in my heart to turn around and see nothing in the space where moments before my dad had been. About the guilt I felt, how I know in my heart that it's my fault, but I can't do anything about it.'

'You were ten years old. It was an accident.'

'I know that now, and in many ways I'm at peace with it. For years I struggled with the guilt, but I'm a grown man and I work in medicine, and I face guilt on a daily basis. Mostly from parents who blame themselves for their children's injuries, or people who've made mistakes while driving, that kind of thing. And I see it for what it is, but I also know from experience that it's not something easily shelved. It stays with you forever.'

Rachel nodded. 'I won't pretend to understand,' she said.

'Thank you. Most people say that they do, but they don't. They can't.'

'I know we don't really know each other,' Rachel said, 'except that I think you're this semi-weirdo who fishes without a line and keeps running off, and you think I'm this semi-weirdo who had a plaster cast when a brace would have done, and who keeps chasing you around with bags of fudge, but if you want to talk about it, I'm happy to listen. And I won't write some sensationalist article and send it to the tabloids. I might have studied journalism, but I'm not a journalist. I work in a fudge and coffee shop.'

William looked up at her and smiled. 'A noble profession,' he said. 'Both of them, if done right. And I think you should try a little harder. I think you'd make a good investigative journalist. You have the right compassion.'

Rachel smiled. 'I'm actually quite enjoying working in the shop. Even if the two old biddies I work with have a little too much interest in my personal life.'

'I imagine it's exciting for them. It's probably been a long time since they were young.'

'They were both teachers.'

'Ah, in that case they were never young. They were born old and strict, like all teachers. I think they make them in a factory somewhere, and fake their pasts so that we believe they're actually human.'

'I think you're spot on.'

They were both quiet for a while. Rachel stared at the little pile of stones on the promontory, and the plate placed in front. The wind ruffled tufts of couch grass that had grown up around it, and the roar of the sea was a constant companion and it pressed and pulled on the rocks below.

'You built that, didn't you?'

'I go out there once a month,' William said. 'I place another little stone.' He shrugged. 'So I can't really talk to you about danger, since I come down here all the time.'

'Why do you sit on the breakwater?' Rachel asked. 'If you don't mind me asking?'

William sighed. 'For years I never really believed that he was gone, like, by some miracle, he had actually survived, and been washed up somewhere, and was perhaps living in a local village under a different identity, having forgotten who he was. I used to walk around all the local villages, looking at people, just in case. I know it was stupid, but I couldn't help myself. It was my way of dealing with it. And then one day, I was by the harbour in Porth Melynos, when the sun was going down.' He smiled. 'I was just standing there, and I looked down, and there was my father's hat, lying half submerged in the silt.'

'Oh my god.'

'I was shocked, of course, but it was weird. I didn't feel any of that sadness that I had expected, but rather I felt a kind of calm, you know? Like part of him, in some way, was actually there. Like he'd chosen it for his final resting place. So I started to go down there and fish off the breakwater, just to be near him.'

'So that's why. But what about … you don't have any line.'

William chuckled. 'Yeah, well, I used to, but since I was just there to be at peace and be near my dad and all that, I didn't really care whether I caught anything. Over the back there, all the serious guys were fishing, so I didn't want to get in their way. I had my line in the water under the breakwater on the landward side, where there are just a few minnows and some crabs, apparently, then one day this Lakes and Fisheries or whatever inspector shows up and tells me I need a fishing license. I said I was sea fishing, for which you don't need a license, but he got a strop on and said that anything inside the breakwater was still part of the river, and therefore I needed a license.' William grinned. 'The guy was a total shark. So I cut the line and told him to stuff his license. He's come back three times since, and each time I've smugly pointed out that I'm not actually fishing, but sitting there, enjoying the fresh air. He checks my rod every time.'

'Sounds like he's keen to catch you.'

'We're all fishermen in our way, aren't we?'

Rachel just nodded. She wanted to say something important, but instead found herself muttering in a quiet voice, almost too quiet to be heard over the wind: 'Would you like to go fishing together sometime?'

And William, turning towards her, met her eyes, at first unsmiling, but then, with a smile spreading across his face, answered, 'I'd like that. But maybe in a river or a lake somewhere, where neither of us have any emotional baggage.'

'We'll just have to keep our heads down and make sure we don't bump into the inspector.'

William smiled. 'Sounds like a plan.'

18

A SURPRISE PROPOSAL

'You're a little perkier this morning,' Clara said, taking a freshly washed cup out of the dishwasher and putting it up on a shelf behind the counter. 'Did you win the lottery?'

Rachel couldn't keep the smile off her face. 'I'm going fishing this afternoon,' she said.

'And you're happy?' Valerie said, one eyebrow perched high on her forehead like a slug that had got lost. 'I'd be crying into my fudge.'

Clara gave her sister a knowing smile. 'Look at her, you idiot. She's not going alone, is she?'

Valerie turned on Rachel. 'Are you not?'

'Ah, not exactly….'

'You're stalking someone?'

'No! It's a … an, um, an … arrangement.'

'Is your companion female, male, neither or both?' Clara asked.

'Because that would define the exact definition of your … excursion,' Valerie added.

'Ah … male,' Rachel said.

'A date,' Clara and Valerie intoned at the same time, then added an extended, 'Ummmm,' which made Rachel smile.

'It's not like that. We're just friends.'

'All relationships start as just friends,' Valerie said. 'Well, myself and my dear departed Ernest actually started as enemies. He pushed me off the slide in playschool, so I threw sand in his face and put a worm in his soup, and our love blossomed from there.'

'Hard to break a bond formed by worms,' Clara said.

'Did he … eat the worm?'

'I think he had a nibble before he realised it wasn't a bit of mushroom, then it was all waterworks and bowls being throw about. My mum took me over and made me apologise, and that was the start of a beautiful hatred that lasted up until we were about sixteen, and then … well, you know how it goes.'

'Do we?' Clara asked.

'Instead of the vixen he'd always seen me as, wily and cunning and intent on his personal destruction, he started to view me as a bit of a fox.' Valerie gave a nostalgic sigh and smiled. 'And then, well, we started channeling our energies into something more productive.'

'We don't need to know more,' Clara said, clapping her hands over her ears.

'I think I'll go and mop out the toilets,' Rachel added. 'Since we're not busy.'

'Five children,' Valerie said, throwing her arms out wide like a stage actress about to launch into song. 'And it might have been five more had my view on the monsters not been soured somewhat by qualifying as a teacher. Honestly, in those early days it was like living with a bulldozer with no handbrake. I was practically turned inside out.'

'Please stop,' Clara said.

'Five children, and do you know how many of them sent me a Christmas card last year?'

'Uh ... all five?'

Valerie clapped a hand on Clara's shoulder. 'Well, yes, that's technically true, but for dramatics sake, let's say none.'

'None?' Rachel said with a smile. 'How ungrateful.'

'Quite, quite,' Valerie said. 'Now, what time is your date?'

'Can't we just say event or appointment?' Rachel asked with a shy smile.

'You are neither a group tour nor sick,' Valerie said. 'Now, Clara and I will prepare a little box of snacks for you to take with you. You know what they say about men, don't you? Keep their—'

'I'm going to mop the toilets!' Rachel said in a voice that was almost jarringly high-pitched, fleeing from the two old women before her ears could be damaged forever, and the likelihood of sleep without troublesome dreams reduced from fifty percent to none.

∽

Chad Evans.

Her father. Rachel gave the library a long look as she waited across the street for William. More than two weeks now she'd kept hold of the card her mother had given her and done absolutely nothing. October's breezy, showery days had given way to November's standing cold, morning mist, and shorter evenings. The leaves had all turned now, and each gust of wind sent brown and orange showers across the car park. Some trees were already bare, their skeletal branches clacking together, and

Rachel's hands spent more time in her coat pockets than out.

Maybe she was just coming to terms with knowing her father's name. Perhaps there was a sense of disappointment that he had seemingly shown an interest in her as a child before immediately disappearing the moment he found out she was actually his. And there was of course the shock that his company was in the same town in which she had been living until recently. While she had no memory of it, having never had to purchase a carpet, she could have walked past it on countless occasions. What if, on one of those times, her father had been outside, washing the windows or picking the weeds out of the pavement, and she had passed within an arm's length of him? It didn't bear thinking about.

'Are you ready?' said a voice behind her, and she jumped to find William stepping up onto a pavement behind her, as silently as cat.

'I didn't see you,' she said. 'You're pretty good at sneaking up on people.'

'I waved to you from across the street, but you were miles away,' William said. Then, holding her gaze, he added, 'You were kind enough to listen to my secrets. Maybe sometime I can listen to yours.'

She was desperate to share with him what she knew about her father, but she didn't have the nerve to say anything. Instead, she gave a shy laugh and lifted the fishing rod she had borrowed from Simon in the pub.

'I'm ready,' she said.

They headed across the street and walked up the path alongside the river until the tarmac gave way to gravel and then to dry, stony earth. With the assurance of someone who knew what they were doing, William led them almost to where the path split from the river to follow a footpath across fields, climbing over a fence into the crispy undergrowth on the other side.

'Isn't that private property?' Rachel asked.

'It is,' William said. 'The next mile or so of forest on the west side of the river is privately owned, and unauthorised persons could be fined.' He tapped a dirty sign half covered by brambles. 'It says so right here.'

'Well, then shouldn't we….'

William smiled. 'It's all right. It's mine.'

'Yours?'

He nodded. 'I own quite a bit of woodland. It's something of a hobby. I like the quiet places for my own use, and it also gives me the opportunity to protect them.' He tapped another sign, even more covered with brambles, a little further along. Through green moss and lichen, Rachel read: BEHAVE YOURSELVES, TAKE HOME YOUR LITTER, AND THE OWNER PROBABLY WON'T MIND.

'There's a lovely pool just up ahead,' William said.

After wading through an area of undergrowth William repeatedly muttered about getting after with a strimmer, they came to a pretty clearing. Here the river widened as it arced around a buttress of rocks and tree roots on the other bank, leaving a wide pool with a sandy area on the west side.

'You can swim in it in the summer,' William said. 'It's not very deep, but it's lovely on a hot day. I wouldn't advise it now, though.'

They set down their stuff on a grassy patch just back from the pool. Rachel hadn't been fishing since a brief, unsuccessful school trip ten years ago, when, to the best of her memory, all she'd caught was a Coke can and a cold, but William was a willing and able teacher as he showed her how to string her line, attach a piece of bait to the hook—William had brought slices of cooked sausage, much to Rachel's relief, having braced herself the whole way for maggots—then cast the line into the water.

'Are we likely to catch anything?' she said, after her third or fourth unsuccessful cast.

William just grinned. 'We might, or we might not. For some fishermen, that's important, for others, not so much. It's about the peace and the calm, and sometimes the company.'

'Thank you for bringing me.'

'I've been looking forward to it all week.'

Rachel felt a little knot in her stomach. William, when he wasn't running away or sneaking up on her, seemed rather nice. He had a serenity about him that she liked, and an openness about his personality—now that she had got through the resistant outer shell—that made her feel like she could tell him anything.

'Really?'

He nodded. 'Yes. I mean, I thought you were really weird at first, but … you know, now I … kind of like you.'

'Ah, thanks.' Her cheeks had to be glowing like an autumn apple, but William was sitting on a fold-out chair a little in front of hers. 'Don't you … have to work today?'

'I only work three days a week,' William said. 'I also do one night shift, and I'm on call a couple of days. I made a point of not overloading myself, though. I earn enough as it is. I don't need a massive salary to be happy. How about you? Are you going to move back to the smoke and look for your big journalism job?'

Rachel shrugged. 'I don't know. I haven't really decided. I wasn't expecting to be back here, so I guess I'll see how it goes. There's still some sorting out to do up at my grandmother's house, and it's a lot for my mum to do on her own.'

'Your grandmother died?'

'Yes, in September.'

'I'm sorry, I didn't know.'

Rachel couldn't remember if she'd told him or not, but figured she'd been more intent on rooting out William's secrets than revealing her own.

'It's okay. She was pretty old. It was harder on my mum, but she's coping admirably well. She's not one to look back. She's always been a forward thinker.'

'Your grandmother was on your father's side?'

'No.' Rachel was silently begging him to ask about her father. 'My mother's side. She was my only real grandparent, because my grandfather died before my mother was even born, and I never knew my grandparents on my father's side.'

Although I might have passed them on the streets of Brentwell a thousand times.

'That's too bad. Those on my father's side died young, and on my mother's side they retired to Spain about ten years ago. They come back once in a while.'

'It must have been hard on your mother without them. Especially with … with your father.'

'My mother died before they left. Cancer. She lived just long enough to see me qualify as a doctor.'

Rachel didn't know where to look. 'I'm sorry,' she said.

William shrugged. 'It is what it is. I used to blame myself for that too, thinking it was caused by the stress of dealing with my father's disappearance, but she was happy in her last years. I'm at peace with it.'

Rachel said nothing. She stared out at the water, at her line bobbing gently in the water.

'You must think I have more baggage than the average cargo plane,' William said.

'It's not that. I—'

Her line bobbed again.

'I think you've caught something,' William said.

The line suddenly cut across the surface of the water, the rod jerking in Rachel's hand.

'Don't let go of it!'

'What do I do?'

'Hold it steady. Don't pull on the line too hard. Just gently.'

'It's moving too much! Help me!'

Rachel stood up and took a couple of steps closer to the riverbank. As she implored William with her eyes, he got up from his chair and came around behind her, wrapping his arms around hers to take hold of the rod. He felt warm against her back, his breath close to her ear. One hand closed over the rod handle, close enough that the sides of their hands were touching.

'Gently, gently. Give him some slack, let him tire himself out.'

Rachel could barely think about the fish with William so close. She only had to turn her head and she would practically be able to—

'That's it, reel him in.'

William released his hold on her as Rachel reeled in the little fish, excited and disappointed at the same time. William took the line and held up the bobbing creature for her to see.

'It's a trout,' he said. 'About fifteen centimetres. Do you want to take him home for dinner, or put him back?'

Rachel smiled. 'I couldn't possibly eat him,' she said. 'Plus, I brought some snacks, courtesy of the two old ladies I work for.'

William nodded. 'I'll put him back then. Don't worry, I can get the hook out gently. We'll come back and see how big he is again next year.'

The near-subliminal allusion to a longer term relationship almost passed Rachel by, but as her brain caught up with William's words she found herself frozen, unable to reply. She stared at his back, mouth gaping fishlike, before regaining herself just in time to mutter, 'That would be nice.'

William removed the fish from the hook and let it free into the water. When he turned back, he was smiling, his eyes eager.

'So … you said you had snacks?'

'Yes, I—'

Rachel paused. From out of the trees on the other side of the river drifted excited laughter. Rachel glanced at William, who gave her a bemused look and lifted a finger to his lips.

'This is silly,' came a high-pitched, excited voice.

'I know a good spot,' came a man's voice, as someone stumbled in the undergrowth, creating a shudder of branches and a burst of laughter.

'I think my leg's stuck!'

'Don't worry, I'm a fireman.'

Two figures appeared out of the trees across the river, one helping the other. Both were clearly drunk, stumbling and laughing with each step. A branch snapped back, knocking one into the other, and both stumbled forward, through the last curtain of undergrowth shielding them from view.

William had started to back away from the riverbank, but it was too late for them to hide. The two figures made their way to the water's edge, where the man turned and put his arms on the woman's shoulders, before taking a step back and dropping to one knee.

'I know we've only known each other for a few days—well, romantically at least—it's obviously been a lot longer than that—but I'm as sure about this as I've ever been about anything. Linda Castle … will you be my wife?'

Rachel stared as her mother, a twig sticking out of her hair and a bramble running up the back of her sweater like a power cable, cupped her face with her hands, and cried out, in a shrill, near-hysterical voice, 'Oh, Colin … yes!'

As Colin Ubbers stood up and ran forward to embrace his new fiancée, catching his foot on a root and literally falling into her arms, Rachel flapped an arm at William, hoping to signal that they should make a speedy exit. However, perhaps misunderstanding, William instead turned, cleared his throat and began to clap.

'Congratulations!'

Linda let out a shriek of horror and pushed Colin away. He stepped back, his foot slipping in the mud along the riverbank. With a gasp his foot plunged down through muck to splash in the water, leaving him with one bent knee up on the bank in a cartoonish déjà vu of the scene that had just occurred.

Catching sight of Rachel, first Linda's eyes widened, then a smile spread across her face.

'Oh, hello dear. Didn't expect to see you here. I hope we're not disturbing something.'

Rachel ignored a quizzical look from William, suppressed a sigh, and said, 'Hello, Mum. I wasn't expecting to see you here either.'

19
PUTTING THE PAST TO REST

WITH A SERIES OF COUNTERTOP NOTES, LONG WALKS, and extra work shifts, Rachel managed to avoid her mother for the next few days. Linda, however, didn't seem all that hung up about it, if the sound of singing in the shower, whistling while she made breakfast, and awkward if extravagant dance steps on the pavement outside (seen, of course, from behind the corner of a tweaked curtain), were anything to go by.

Objectively, of course, Rachel was distraught at the prospect of becoming Cathy's stepsister, not to mention step-aunt, or step-half-sister, or step-half-(god)-mother/overlord (or something else she would need to Google in order to find out) of baby Raquel. The prospect of seeing even more of Gavin than she already did was unappealing too, even if it was tempered somewhat by her fledging relationship with William.

Really, she didn't want to think about it, but with no money or car she had no way of escaping from Porth Melynos for a few days, and with William informing her that he had to work extra shifts over the coming weekend, she was stuck with trying to keep her head down in the café. Of course, in small villages, news travelled fast.

'So … do you think you'll be a bridesmaid?' Clara asked, stirring a cup of coffee with a plastic spoon, head cocked as she watched Rachel with amused interest.

'I have no idea.'

'But it's possible, isn't it?'

'Look, I know my personal life is like an ongoing soap opera for you two—'

Clara gave a little titter. 'We were delighted to offer you extra shifts. Who needs the telly when we have you?'

Rachel rolled her eyes. 'Glad to be of service.'

'So … have you called the carpet seller yet?'

With a grimace, Rachel shook her head. 'I can't bring myself to. I'm … scared.'

'Why don't you go up there and just, you know, walk past a couple of times?'

Valerie came out of the kitchen. 'And then when that dastardly old fool comes out, you give him a piece of your mind. Calls himself a father—'

'I don't know what to do. I wish I could just forget I'd ever asked about him. He's never been in my life, and I was happy, you know? It didn't matter. Now I've made a big deal of it, and it's like a lump stuck in my throat that I can't get out.'

'You have to find closure,' Clara said. 'You know that, don't you?'

'I—'

The door flew open with a rattle of the bell. Cathy, wearing only a dressing gown that was short enough to expose legs as thick as Rachel's chest, exploded into the room.

'O.M.G. I've been out of town, and now I'm back. I had to see you. Sister.'

'Technically they're still engaged—'

'It's like a book, isn't it? Us coming together like this. I mean, Mum's not all that pleased about it, but she said she's cool with coming to the wedding, and it's just going to be awesome. One big happy family. You know, we have to go shopping. We need matching dresses. I was thinking that we could both hold one handle of Raquel's pram. I mean, you're not her mother, but you've been there since the beginning, haven't you?'

'Uh huh,' Rachel said.

'Dad's so happy. And he's so cool. You'll finally have a dad.'

'Yeah—'

Valerie held up the phone. 'Rachel, call for you. It's William.'

Rachel hadn't heard the phone ring, and from her expression, clearly neither had Clara. Rachel gave Valerie a grateful nod and took it, but before she'd even put it to her ear, Cathy grabbed her hair with both hands and let out the kind of wail that in past years might have brought the nuthouse van screeching through the streets.

'No. No! You haven't got a boyfriend. Oh, you have! This is perfect. We can double date. Actually, what are you doing this Saturday? Come round. Gavin can get to know John, or what was his name?'

'William.'

'And you can spend some time playing with Raquel while they drink beer and gamble. I can't wait. I'll be back later with a time. O.M.G!'

Cathy retreated backwards through the door like someone being sucked into a time portal. Clara pulled the door shut and turned the closed sign round before Cathy could think of something further to say. With a sigh, Rachel lifted the phone to her ear, only to hear the buzz of a dialing tone. She glanced at Valerie, who shrugged.

'It was worth a try,' she said.

～

After her shift ended, Rachel headed down to the harbour. She walked out along the breakwater, watching the fishermen for a few minutes, then headed up the hill to her grandmother's house. After failing to find any photographs of her father, she had lost her motivation to sort through her grandmother's things, and had left the rest for her mother, only helping with the moving of a few last pieces of furniture. However, at the sight of the estate agent's van outside, and someone wandering around in the garden with a clipboard, she felt a sudden lurch in her heart.

It was only a house, she reminded herself. What had made it special was no longer there.

She sat down on the curb outside. A few minutes later, when the estate agent came out, he gave her no more than a polite nod before getting into his van and driving away. Another large slice of the past-pie about to be hacked off and thrown into the river. Rachel squeezed her eyes shut, trying to resist an urge to be sick.

It was only a house. It was surely only a house.

Just like Porth Melynos was only a place, one she could easily leave behind.

Wasn't it?

～

Of all the people to see on her walk back down to the port, Gavin was the last she would have expected. He was standing on the breakwater, wrapping a mooring line around a bollard while his father's fishing boat bobbed in the water. He saw Rachel coming and waved a hand in acknowledgement as she approached, but said nothing until she had stopped in front of him.

'How are you doing?' he said, years falling off his face, restoring him to the Gavin of old who had waved her off on the bus for the last time, tears in his eyes, his forced smile blowing off the last vestiges of their relationship. It had hollowed out a young Rachel at the core, but there had been no going back. She had cried all the way to Exeter, but had stepped off the bus into a new world and new life. There had been no tearful phone calls or even a drunken text. It had been over, and both had drawn a clear line in the seaweed-strewn Porth Melynos shingle.

Now, looking at him again without the lumbering presence of Cathy or Valerie and Clara chirping at her shoulder, she saw an older, wiser Gavin, but one now content with his position in life and at ease with the choices he had made. There was a hint of regret in his eyes, as there surely was in hers, but it was held in check by the new framework he had built around himself. There would be no affairs or rash decisions to run off and leave his children with the return of an old flame; their relationship was over and there was no going back. However, there was no way to erase what had passed between them, the three years of teenage thrill and bliss they had shared before it all came crashing down, and in Gavin's presence she still felt the freedom to talk like she always had.

'I'm not doing so well,' she said.

He nodded at the line of cafés and trinket shops along the harbour's eastern side.

'When I'm done with this rope I'll have time for coffee,' he said.

~

It wasn't raining. The wind wasn't ripping slates off the roofs and smashing them like firecrackers in the streets. It wasn't even that cold, and the leafless trees along the harbourside stood like quiet, skeletal sentinels as a young waitress brought two large coffees over to the window table Rachel and Gavin shared.

'It must have been hard to come back here,' Gavin said. 'I think we both realised there were two groups of people in school, those who'd leave and never come back, and those who'd stay and never leave. You either love the life here or you don't.'

Rachel sighed. 'I never planned to come back,' she said. 'If Grandma hadn't died, I don't think I would have. Mum had trained me so well to always be thinking of the future. I just don't think I did a very good job of it, and sometimes what you plan in life isn't what life has planned out for you.'

Gavin smiled. 'You know, it took me years to get over you. You have no idea how many times I'd come out of the pub at half past eleven and feel the urge to message you.'

'You'd have to have walked halfway up the cliff to get a signal.'

Gavin laughed. 'Believe it or not, I did a couple of times.' He shook his head. 'But then I'd sit there with my phone in my hand, your number on the screen in front of me, and I knew it wasn't what either of us really wanted.'

Rachel nodded. 'I did the same thing. More than a few times. There was once I threw my phone into a hedge to stop myself messaging you. It took three hours to find it the next morning. I had a massive hangover too.'

'What we had … it was awesome. But it would never

have lasted. We were too different. I knew that when we got together but I hoped, you know.'

'It shouldn't have to be this way, should it?'

Gavin shrugged. 'Sometimes it does. Before you came back here for your grandmother, how often did you think about me? Be honest.'

Rachel frowned. She understood what he was trying to say, and why. Coming back here, seeing him again, finding out he had children with Cathy Ubbers of all people, it had started cannons firing all over again. But had she never come back here at all—

'There was always going to be a part of me that still loved you,' she said. 'But I was at peace with it. It was over. I'd even had a couple of boyfriends, although they didn't last very long. But you're right. I was over you. I suppose I thought about you from time to time, but it was more like going through old photographs. I knew it could never be how it was. I mean, I wasn't expecting that you would have shacked up with Cathy Ubbers—'

Gavin shrugged and gave a sly smile that told Rachel far more than his words could have done. 'That wasn't part of my plan either, but sometimes things just happen, don't they?'

'Like my grandmother dying, meaning I have to come back here and face all the demons that are holding me back in life?'

'Something like that. Have you faced them yet?'

Rachel looked out of the window at the harbour. Not so much had changed after all, now that she thought about it. Her roots were systematically being pulled up one by one and thrown into the water, but otherwise, Porth Melynos was the same place she had grown up in, and the same place she had left. Only the faces had changed, or aged, or left.

She looked back at Gavin. 'I'm in the process of doing so,' she said. 'When I first came back and saw you, my heart skipped a beat. Then I found out about Cathy, and I realised you'd moved on. I wasn't sure when I first came back, but I'm over you, Gavin.'

Gavin nodded. 'And that's the way it's supposed to be, isn't it?'

'I think it is.'

～

Half an hour later, walking back up the street from the harbour, Rachel found herself smiling. She had declined Gavin's offer of a second coffee and not felt a moment of regret about it. While the awkwardness of being a member of Gavin's extended family might still be on the horizon, their relationship was firmly in the past, and Rachel was at peace with it. She was ready to move forward.

Linda had already gone to work when Rachel got back, and the flat was empty. The light on her mother's slow cooker was the only light glowing in the kitchen, the aroma of a curry filling the little space. A note on the worktop told Rachel she would need to boil some rice but otherwise to help herself. She thought about a glass of wine, but decided to get the phone call out of the way first.

It would be easy to send a message, but since leaving Gavin, Rachel had felt an overwhelming urge to hear another voice. She dialed the number, pressed the old headset to her ear, and hoped William would answer.

Five rings. An automated message started, and Rachel's heart sank. She waited, listening to the beginnings of a pre-recorded message, and was about to hang up when the message abruptly cut off and William's voice said, 'Hello?'

Rachel's hands tingled, and her cheeks flushed. 'It's Rachel,' she said.

'Hi!' the sudden enthusiasm in his voice told her all she needed to know.

'What are you up to?'

'Oh, you know, the usual. Just starting a night shift, but I'll be off at midnight. Will that be too late to call?'

'Depends on what film I watch and whether it makes me fall asleep.'

'I'll try anyway.'

Rachel smiled into the phone. 'I'll stuff matchsticks into my eyes to keep myself awake.'

'I have Monday and Tuesday off next week, if you wanted to do something. Perhaps we should hold off on the fishing for a while. Or at least go somewhere a little more open, so we can run away if your mother shows up.'

'Actually … there was something I was wondering if you could help me with.'

'What's that?'

Rachel took a deep breath. 'I need to talk to you about someone I've not told you about.'

'Sure. Who?'

'My … dad.'

20

CARPETS NEW AND OLD

It felt a little strange to be back in Brentwell again. As Rachel got down from the bus, she felt a moment of trepidation, but then William's hand touched her shoulder.

'You'll need to take a couple more steps,' he said. 'If you stay there, the bus can't leave.'

'Sorry.' Rachel stumbled forward. 'I'm just a little nervous.'

William climbed down behind her, and they walked together over to the small bus station as the bus pulled away.

'Are you hungry?' he asked. 'We can get a sandwich or something.'

Rachel shook her head. 'I can't. I'm too nervous. What if this is the day I finally meet my dad, and he doesn't want to know?'

William gave her shoulder a tentative pat. 'One step at a time,' he said. 'Let's find this carpet place first and take it from there.'

Rachel had the business card in her purse, but the

address was already imprinted on her mind. A brief look at the town map behind a Perspex screen inside the terminal told her exactly where to find it.

'It's right round the corner from the chippy me and Bethany used to go to on a Friday,' she said to William as he returned from the little newsagent on the corner, having decided to buy a couple of sandwiches just in case Rachel changed her mind. 'There was an off-license up that road we sometimes went to. I must have walked past that shop a dozen times.'

'Young people don't tend to think about carpets unless they spill something,' William said with an amused smirk. 'Shall we go and take a look?'

Rachel took a deep breath. 'Okay. Let's get this over with.'

∼

She was fine until they got to the corner of Fore Street. The chippy she had once frequented was now nothing more than a faded sign above boarded-up windows, a recent change that felt like a glaring metaphor warning her away. As William walked on round the corner, she stopped, feet taking root, unable to bring herself to move another step.

William paused at the corner and looked back.

'It's okay,' he said. 'We don't have to do this if you don't want to.'

Rachel stared at him as he walked back to her. 'I really want to do this,' she said. 'I'm just utterly terrified.'

'That's natural.'

'Shall we get coffee?'

Rachel nodded. 'I think that's a good idea.'

Not far from Fore Street was the entrance to Sycamore

Park, where Rachel had sometimes gone on a Saturday to meet friends or have picnics. It was blustery and cold now, the tall sycamores that lined the path mostly devoid of leaves, the branches swaying in the occasional gusts of wind that rattled through the park, making Rachel zip the fluffy lining tight around her neck and stuff her hands deep into her jacket pockets. William stood beside her, sheltering her a little as a smiling man in a burger van by the park's southern entrance handed them two large paper cups of coffee. Together they walked around the park, past a rippling duck pond and the local theatre, then out past a closed café by the northern entrance. They talked about nothing while they drank their coffee, commentating on the weather, interesting shops they passed, whether they thought it would snow this year, anything in fact to avoid the pressing subject at hand. Until, finally, they found themselves once more on the corner of Fore Street.

'We can do another coffee circuit if you like,' William said. 'Although I'd prefer to sit down somewhere for a bit.'

Rachel shook her head. 'I'm ready.'

'Are you sure?'

'No. But keep walking and I'll try to follow you.'

William reached out an arm. 'Let's do it together.'

Rachel stared at it for a moment, then hooked her arm through his. He eased her closer, and it felt nice, safe. Rachel felt a little shiver that wasn't from the cold.

'Thank you,' she said.

'Shall we?'

She nodded. 'Okay.'

They walked around the corner. From the way the street arced, Chad Evans' Carpeting and Upholstery seemed to be running away from them, forever out of sight as the property numbers ticked by. Up ahead on the opposite side, the off-license she had occasionally visited was already visible, so she must have passed these buildings dozens of times. 4 … 6 … 8 … 10 … it wouldn't be there. It had to have closed down years ago, turned into an innocuous accountant or a lawyer's office, the eye sliding over it without a second glance. 12 …

14.

Carpeting and Upholstery.

C&A Evans Associates.

And there, underneath, in swirly writing across frosted glass, the infamous catchphrase: *You'll N'Evans find a better carpet.*

An open sign hung on the door, but times must have been hard, because several letters in the catchphrase had faded or peeled away, so a casual eye would read it as *You'll N'Evans find a better cat*, making Rachel wonder if a little diversification into the pet market might not be a good idea.

'Shall we go inside?'

Rachel was still staring at the shop front, a narrow space between a residential house and a dentist. The blurry ghosts of carpet rolls were just visible through the frosted windows, the door slightly ajar, perhaps catching on a wooden step that needed repainting. She started to shake her head, then stopped.

'Now or never,' she said.

William, clearly sensing her unease, went first, holding the door for Rachel to come in behind. No bell tinkled, and they were immediately surrounded by towering, tree-like carpet rolls of all manner of colours, and a musty, nose-clogging smell that felt like having lumps of thread stuffed up your nostrils. William, perhaps used to far worse in the hospital, didn't seem concerned, but Rachel puffed breath out of her mouth to avoid using her nose. She felt in a veritable jungle, lost, overwhelmed, disorientated, but when she turned to look for the door, she found only more carpet rolls behind her, as though they had been sucked into an alternative upholstery world and there was no way back out.

'Hello!' came a sudden voice so jarring in its cheerfulness that Rachel backed into a stack of rugs and might have rolled over backwards had William not reached out a steadying hand. The man who appeared through a gap in the carpet trees was like something out of a comedy movie. He had a bushy mop of hair, sideburns that covered his ears, and wore an orange sweater that could have come from a low budget fruit advert. As Rachel's thundering heart began to slow, she tried to focus on the man's eyes and smile, wondering if she'd seen them before.

'Are you looking for anything in particular? We have a wide selection of rugs and throws if you still prefer the floorboard look. Or there's plenty of fitted options if you're more traditional. What depth of pile are you after?'

Rachel tried to find her voice, but no words would come out. The longer she looked at the man, the more she was convinced, however, that this was not her father. He wasn't old enough for a start, barely older than William, despite a retro look that wouldn't have looked out of place in a 1970s sitcom.

'Actually, we were looking for Chad Evans,' Rachel managed to stutter at last. 'Are you him?'

The man's eyes widened. 'Chad? Wow, there's a name I've not heard in a while.'

'Is he ... here?'

'Good heavens, no. He's long gone, I'm afraid, up to the great upholsterers in the sky. Must be nearly twenty years now.'

Rachel sagged. William caught her, propping her back up as she muttered, 'Oh. That's too bad.'

'Were you friends?'

'My mother … knew him.'

The man let out a chuckle. 'Chad, gosh. Your mother wasn't a customer, was she? We used to joke that he had a woman in every town. Quite the travelling salesman, was Chad.'

Rachel would have sagged again had William not still held her. Her legs and arms felt like jelly, her mouth full of fuzz.

'So he's dead?'

'I'm afraid so.'

Rachel had wondered how this moment might feel. In many ways, it was almost a relief. The years during which she had needed a father the most were already gone, and rediscovering him now would have required driving a wedge into her life, one which might not have been either wanted or needed. Even so, it was a shock. She had wanted to look him in the eyes, even if it was just one time.

'You're his … son?'

'Nephew. The name's Todd. Todd Evans. My dad—Chad's brother—wasn't well enough to take over the business, so I took it on.' He spread his arms. 'It might not look like much, but most of what we do is online these days. You're my first customers this week. In the store at least.' He chuckled and gave a brief, asthmatic cough. 'I wasn't really expecting anyone. Otherwise I might have hoovered. I hope you're thinking of buying something.'

'I could do with a new rug for my office while we're here,' William said, flashing Rachel a smile, then giving her hand a quick squeeze.

'We have a fine selection,' although the better ones are lower down the pile, less sun-faded.' Another chuckle, suggesting a joke. 'What was it you wanted from Chad, by the way? Did he overcharge you? Dad always said he was a fiend for service stations. Used to add a 'service' charge to every bill so he could afford more overpriced coffee and breakfast baps. A real road warrior, was Uncle.'

Rachel cleared her throat.

'I think I might be his daughter,' she said.

21

CLOSURE

'I'VE ONLY GOT PG TIPS,' TODD SAID, GIVING THE POT A shake, a poorly fitting knitted tea cozy with a petrol station logo printed on the side slipping off and on as the pot moved back and forth. 'Coffee plays havoc with my backdoor. I had to have one of those tubes last year, and the doctor suggested a few dietary changes. I miss the shortbread the most, but you know, the sugar. Cracker?' He held out a long, orange packet. Rachel took one, but William declined with thanks. 'And it's oat milk. That okay? Same reason. I went too hard on the lactose in my youth. Used to be a lovely café across the street that did great milkshakes, but it shut a couple of years back. People are all like, 'let's build cow sanctuaries' and all that these days, aren't they?'

'PG Tips is fine,' Rachel said.

'Just fine,' William added, meeting her eyes and giving her a smile.

'So, you're Chad's daughter?' Todd chuckled and rubbed the knees of his corduroy trousers. 'Wow, I never thought I'd see the day. That makes us cousins, you know. I didn't have any when I was a kid. I had to play LEGO on my own, instead of going to sandpits and stuff.'

Rachel nodded, forcing a smile. 'I don't have proof that Chad is my father. It's only what my mother told me. He fitted my grandmother's carpets.'

Todd grinned. 'And your mother fell for that handsome carpet salesman, did she? He was quite the suave talker, so Dad always said. When he started running his mouth, lino would start to curl, wanting to be replaced.'

'How … nice.'

'Honestly, he wasn't that bad. I didn't see him all that much because he was usually out on the road, but he always had a smile and a bit of banter. Must have been fifty people at his funeral.' Todd chuckled again, then ran a hand through his mop of hair, which sprang neatly back into place. 'And not all of them had turned up just to make sure he was really dead. A couple of people seemed actually sad.'

'Can I ask how he died?'

Todd leaned forward, his eyes gleaming. 'Right. Well, that's a story in itself. Almost made the regional TV news.'

'Really?'

'Almost. It got pulled at the last minute.'

'Oh?'

Todd shrugged. 'New evidence came to light. We tried to get them to run it anyway—publicity for the shop and all that—but they weren't having it. Said it would damage their reputation.'

'Why?'

'Chad was coming back across Dartmoor one night, in the middle of a ferocious storm. My dad got this message appear on his phone which just made no sense at all. He didn't think anything of it until the next morning, when Chad still wasn't back. Dad called the police, and they eventually found Chad's car, on the side of the road. Chad had died of a heart attack, right there in the car, in the middle of the storm. Quite Shakespearean, isn't it?'

Rachel covered her mouth. 'Oh my god.'

'What did the message say?' William asked.

Todd grinned. 'You'll laugh, but at the time we were convinced. It said, 'The beast! The beast is here!' We didn't get it until they found his camera in the car. He'd got one last grainy photo of something standing on the bonnet of his car.'

Rachel looked at William, then back at Chad. 'The Beast of Dartmoor?'

Todd attempted to click his fingers, but the sound came out as a dull thump. 'Exactly. Naturally, we called the local newspaper and got them to run the story, but by the time the regional TV news became interested, some spoilsport journalist had doused our fire somewhat.'

'How do you mean?'

'Well, close analysis of the photograph, as well as prints found in mud nearby, suggested it wasn't the Beast of Dartmoor after all, but a regular, domestic cat. Possibly not a very big one, maybe even a kitten. My uncle's heart attack was caused by a cat. Such an irony, considering he loved the things. Said they were the only thing softer than a good Chad Evans carpet.'

～

Rachel and William walked back through Sycamore Park. It had started to spit and the wind had got up, but they found the little café by the northern entrance open. A kindly middle-aged lady who introduced herself as Angela brought them two overloaded maple and walnut lattes and two large slices of pecan pie, the last, she said, of the season, before the café closed for the winter. A decent cream and sugar hit made Rachel feel a little better, even if her overall sense of the trip was one of failure.

'At least you've got some kind of closure,' William said.

'I'm sorry. I should be pleased, shouldn't I? At least I know for sure that he's dead.'

'Believe it or not, in time it'll help,' William said. 'In my heart, I know my father's gone. I might not have ever found his body, but I don't need to. I can feel it. When you have that, it makes life easier. At the moment it's like an open wound for you, but give it a few months, and you'll feel better.'

'Is that what you would say to your patients?'

William smiled. 'Mostly. Then I'd tell them to speak to the receptionist about a future appointment. Seriously, though, give it a little time. You'll feel better. You might never get over it completely, however, but that's okay. That's the way things go.'

'Perhaps I'll find myself talking to my grandmother's carpets ... I'm sorry, I didn't mean it like that.'

William patted her hand. 'You don't have to apologise. People deal with their grief in different ways. Some people run away from it. Others try to ignore it. Some embrace it as part of themselves, and learn to live with it.'

Rachel sighed and shook her head. 'I don't know how to feel. It's almost absurd. My father was a carpet salesman killed by a cat.'

'I'm not sure you could say the cat was directly responsible. He probably had a weak heart.'

'Are you trying to cheer me up?'

'I am. I'm not sure if it's working or not.'

'I appreciate the effort. Don't give up.'

Their eyes met again. Underneath her despondency, Rachel felt something a little more positive. Perhaps the world wouldn't collapse in on her completely. Perhaps it would leave a little room for some light, or some air.

'I think it's time we went home,' William said.

They thanked Angela, paid their bill and left. The wind had got up, and evening was drawing in. The man from the burger van who had served them coffees gave them a wave as he fastened down the window side of his van. As flurries of rain began to appear, William wrapped his arm around Rachel to shelter her as they hurried for the bus station.

They arrived only a few minutes before the last bus. While William went to buy some drinks and snacks from the newsagent on the corner, Rachel stood under the bus shelter and looked back up the road in the direction of her father's old shop.

Life felt heavy, the seasons' turn a burden upon her shoulders. The future felt uncertain, like a mystery carpet yet to unroll.

'Goodbye, Dad,' she whispered.

22

WINDFALL

'Who's going to want fudge at six o'clock?' Valerie said, waving her arms at Clara. 'Four o'clock, I'm telling you. We'll only be wasting electric if we stay open longer.'

'But what about the post-work crowd?'

'They'll have to get used to it. Or nip out at lunchtime. This is fudge and postcards we're talking about, not milk and toilet roll.'

Rachel only half listened as the two old ladies argued about closing times. With November on the downward slide and Christmas lights already appearing further down the street, Clara was insistent that there would be a winter boom, while Valerie wanted to close up and be done with it. In truth, the shop was empty for most of the day now, their only customers a handful of elderly people on autumn holidays, of which most of whom shouldn't be eating too much fudge anyway. They still did okay with the coffees in the mid-afternoon, but they were probably spending more on heating than they were making. Rachel's hours had been cut back to just four per day, three days a week, and she spent much of the rest of her time moping about at home, struggling to find direction in her life.

'All right, four,' Clara said with a dramatic huff. 'But six on Saturdays.'

'You can work that shift then,' Valerie said.

'I can do it,' Rachel said.

The two old ladies glanced at each other.

'Ah ... that was something else,' Clara said.

'Yes,' Valerie agreed. 'Would you be okay if we just cut you back to lunchtimes? You see, we don't really need so many staff at this time of year.'

'Sorry, dear,' Clara said. 'It's a purely economic thing.'

Rachel just gave a dumb nod. 'Sure.'

'I heard from Benny that they're looking for someone in the pub,' Clara said. 'If you're after more work, you could have a word. Everyone knows you after all.'

'I suppose.'

'Or you could diversify,' Valerie said. 'Isn't it this time of year people start delivering phonebooks?'

'Do people still use phonebooks?' Clara said.

'How would I know?' Valerie shrugged. 'Or perhaps you could start a YouTube channel?'

'My mum's internet isn't strong enough to run it,' Rachel heard herself say in a wistful, faraway voice, as though the emotional part of her was already running, sprinting down to the harbour to douse itself in cold, wintery water.

'Things will pick up in the new year,' Clara said. 'Once it starts getting light.'

'It is a little depressing at this time of year,' Valerie added. 'The long evenings and the rain, and all that.'

Rachel felt the sudden urge to cry. Everything felt hopeless. She wanted to call William, but he was doing extra work shifts at the hospital. Doctors liked to go on holiday at this time of year, he told her, and there were a lot more minor injuries caused by slipping in the wind and rain.

'Are you sure you're all right, dear?' Clara asked.

Rachel opened her mouth to speak, but before any words could come out, the door burst open, and Cathy Ubbers stood there, dramatic and windswept, her hair billowing out behind her massive body like a sentinel holding back the elements.

'You'll never guess what's happened,' she said, looking from one to the other.

'You're pregnant yet again?' Clara said.

'You're moving to Australia?' Valerie added.

Cathy grinned and shook her head. 'You're both wrong. O.M.G. I just won the Lottery.' She spread her arms wide. 'Can you believe it? Little old nobody me just became a millionaire!'

'O.M.G.,' Rachel muttered, hoping she didn't sound too sarcastic.

'I can't believe it,' Cathy said. 'Gav's at home ordering in the champagne. You will come to the pub tonight, won't you? All drinks are free.' She gave a phlegmy chuckle. 'Well, not free, but on us.' She looked at Rachel and winked. 'There might even be sausage rolls.'

While Rachel was still trying to figure out how the presence of sausage rolls might be of particular interest to her, Cathy grabbed both edges of the door frame and began to shake back and forth.

'Yee hah! We're rich! Oh, what a day! And it was only a Lucky Dip. It's a miracle. O.M. … G!'

'Quite,' Valerie said. 'What are you going to spend your money on?'

Cathy gave a shudder as though throwing off a ghost, then looked at Valerie and grinned. 'I've already put an offer in for the launderette,' she said. 'You have to invest in business, don't you? Can't just throw your money away.'

'For sure,' Valerie said with a subtle roll of her eyes. 'A sound investment, that.'

'And we were thinking of moving into somewhere a little bigger,' Cathy said. 'Especially with the kids growing so fast. Although of course they'll now be going to private boarding schools. I'll need a reflection room, though.'

'A what?'

'And a powder room. And Gav might want a study, or a games room. A man-cave where he can play poker with his mates. You can't do these things with a simple two-up, two-down.'

'No,' Valerie agreed, while Clara just chuckled.

'You need a lot more space.'

Rachel had been hoping to dissolve, but even as she stepped back behind the counter, hoping to blend chameleon-like into the background of coffee machines and cupboards, Cathy's gaze turned like a lighthouse beacon towards her, illuminating and holding her in place.

'I can't believe I never thought of it,' Cathy said, eyes widened. 'Is your grandma's place up for sale yet?'

23

TIME TRAVEL

'CAN'T YOU LIVE THERE AFTER YOU MARRY COLIN?'

Linda gave a light titter and shook her head. 'Oh, it wouldn't be practical,' she said. 'We can't be dealing with that hill at our ages. Colin wants to be closer to the shops anyway, so we thought we'd look at a few places in Plymouth.'

'There are shops here!'

'The pasty shop and the rock shop don't really count,' Linda said. 'Why are you so staunchly defending this place anyway? You've been talking about leaving again since the day you came back.'

'I—'

'Just in case, nothing is decided yet. I mean, I might keep our flat to rent out. It just wouldn't be practical to keep your grandmother's house. Not with house prices what they are. Colin said the bubble's about to burst, so we'd be best to sell up now before all the prices come down.'

'But—'

'Oh, Rachel, you're still young. When you get to my

age, life has a different perspective. You don't want the struggle anymore. You want a quiet life, one where you have everything you need on your doorstep, where you haven't got to worry about the wind blowing the tiles off the roof, or the drains backing up—'

Linda wandered, still talking, into the kitchen. Rachel stared out of the window, filtering her mother out, wondering what else needed to go wrong. William could ring up and break up with her, she supposed, although she wasn't even sure they were more than friends. He hadn't even tried to kiss her yet, something that had been playing on her mind more as the days passed.

Linda reappeared, carrying two cups of tea. 'Oh, did I tell you that I talked to my boss at the hotel? He said they might have some hours in the kitchen if you're desperate.'

'If I'm desperate– '

'It would just be washing up, cleaning, that kind of thing. One of the school kids just quit.' Linda rolled her eyes. 'Little weakling. Said the washing up liquid was giving her a skin condition, making it difficult to hold a pen. We all knew it was just an excuse. She probably wants to spend more time watching Netflix or YouTube.'

'Chance would be a fine thing.'

Linda's eyes widened. 'Oh, and did you hear about Cathy Ubbers? Won two million quid on the National Lottery. Isn't that fantastic?'

'Fantastic,' Rachel muttered.

'Although, you can't buy much with two million quid these days. Still, a nice nest egg for her and Gavin, presuming she doesn't blow it. You should buddy up to her a bit more. She might treat you to lunch.'

Rachel sat down in an armchair as her mother put the cups of tea down on the coffee table.

'I've got to go to work in a bit. There's some Bolognese in the fridge if you want it.'

'Thanks.'

Linda cocked her head. 'Come on, love. Don't look so down in the dumps. Why don't you go down to the pub and have a drink and a chat.'

'It's Thursday night. It'll probably be empty.'

'Well, maybe there's something nice on the telly.'

'I checked. There isn't.'

'What about that boyfriend of yours?'

'He's not my boyfriend, and he's working anyway.'

Linda smiled. 'We really are at the end of the rope, aren't we?'

'Mum … I just feel like I'm going nowhere. Clara and Valerie cut my hours in the café again. I don't have a car, and you're about to make me homeless.'

Linda rolled her eyes and sighed. 'Don't be so dramatic. Even if I put the flat on the market now, it would take months for a sale to go through. You'd have loads of time to find something else.'

'That's reassuring.'

'Come on, didn't I bring up my little girl to be positive? Why don't you do something constructive, like paint a picture or write a book or something?'

Rachel glanced around the room, wondering where she'd left her notebook. She'd done a page or two of a possible article, but that was about it. And it had only been mostly notes. Nothing much. But, with nothing better to do, she supposed she could have another crack at it, even if it was more of a diary than anything else.

'Right,' Linda said, finishing her tea and standing up. 'I'd better get to work. Have a nice evening, and try not to get too down about everything. Tomorrow is a new day, isn't it? But, if you do want to drown your sorrows, there's a tenner in the pot on the kitchen windowsill. You should be able to afford a pint, even at today's prices.'

'Thanks, Mum.'

Linda took her coat off a hook behind the door and swung it over her shoulders. As she glanced back at Rachel, she smiled.

'Don't give up, love,' she said. 'Where's that little girl who was always so positive?'

'She's hiding.'

'Well, go and find her.'

Rachel stared at the back of the door as Linda went out. Her mother was right, it was just that life felt so hard sometimes. Just getting up out of the armchair was a chore, as was walking around the living room in search of her notebook. She had started to write something about William's father and her own, but it had felt stupid, but perhaps she could write something else, about her ex-boyfriend's new soon-to-be wife wanting to buy her grandmother's house and convert the cellar into a powder room or a gambling den. Perhaps she could write a sitcom, if she could find some way to twist her misfortune into humour.

However, as she went from room to room, she failed to find her notebook anywhere. She couldn't remember leaving it at the shop, so she must have dropped it or perhaps left it on the bus to Brentwell.

Taking one last sweep through the kitchen and coming up with nothing, she turned instead to the ten pound note poking out of her mother's sundries jar on the windowsill. She had a tenner of her own, so perhaps she might be able to get just drunk enough to make some sense of her life.

As she had expected, the pub was empty. She ordered a pint, purely because it would take longer to drink, and then sat in a corner while the landlord stood behind the bar, watching an evening football match on the TV. Not really thinking, Rachel had forgotten even to bring her phone, so found herself forced to get into a dull nil-nil match between Watford and West Ham. By half time, the landlord had taken to reading a newspaper, clearly bored.

Finding herself surprisingly still awake when the final whistle went, Rachel was just about to leave when the door opened and Alan Marsh came in. Limping over to the bar, her grandmother's old gardener took up a stool and ordered a pint.

Rachel had skipped dinner, and the pint had left her feeling a little tipsy. She waited until Alan had settled on his stool with a pint in front of him before getting up and wandering over.

'Hey, Alan.'

'Get on, lass. Drinking alone?'

'Not anymore.'

'Well, me luck's in tonight, ain't it?' Alan gave a little chuckle. 'Shouldn't you be out with a younger crowd rather than hanging around an old codger like me?'

Rachel shrugged. 'It's Thursday night.'

'Aye,' Alan said. 'Must be skittles night. Away match.'

'Can I ask you something?'

'Sure, lass. Geoff! Pint for the girl.' As the landlord replaced Rachel's drink, Alan leaned forward. 'What do you want to pick these old weathered brains for?'

'Do you remember when you were working for my grandmother?'

Alan chuckled. 'Just about. Fine old dear was Marigold.'

'Do you ever remember a man coming in to change the carpets?'

Alan frowned for a moment, tapping a gnarled finger on the bar. Just as Rachel was about to give up hope, his eyes widened. 'Ah, him. Yeah, I remember. Odd looking guy, ridiculous hair.'

'Was his name Chad by any chance?'

'Chad?' Alan chuckled. 'We weren't never on no first name terms, but I remember ee. Did them carpets fine like, then kept showing up even after he was done.' He winked. 'Always when your mother was there. Fine piece, was Linda—'

'That's nice,' Rachel said quickly. 'Was I there?'

Alan frowned again. 'Let's have a think ... no ... ah, yeah, I suppose so. All a bit hard to remember, and I weren't there on weekdays, only weekends, see. Not sure what went on otherwise, but she had me cutting in the garden sometimes, with Linda and those legs of hers sitting out on the patio with a cup of tea, and he was there, couple of rolls of carpet standing about for some aesthetic value, but he's down there with a doll in his hands waving it about like he's your dad.'

'While I was there?'

'Well, yeah. He was a bit of a weird so-and-so but he weren't playing dolls on his own, was ee?'

Rachel smiled. 'I thought I'd better check. So he was playing with me?'

'Ah, it was only a couple of times, like. That I saw. I was down there in the garden one time, you know, where you could get the best view of your mother's pegs,'—he let out a chortle, coughing beer across the bar before swiping a sleeve across his face—'and I'm thinking, why doesn't the lazy bugger get on with laying them carpets? You needs a playmate, go up 'hall and join the playgroup.' He shook his head and chuckled. 'Lazy bugger. Some of us had to work for a living.'

Rachel nodded. 'It sounds like you're in the wrong profession.'

Ah, 'twas all me life. Got to spend me time out in the sun, though. Couldn't imagine fitting carpets. Sitting around indoors, kneeling in someone else's dust all day long. How's your mother, by the way?'

'Getting married. To Colin Ubbers.'

Alan chuckled. 'That old fart. Good luck to her. Wouldn't know a good time, would Colin, if it jumped out of a sand trap at one of his golf days and bit him on the saggy backside.'

'You should have been quicker on the draw.'

'Ah, even after me old Maggie's passing, weren't no need for me to reenter that silly old market,' Alan said. His eyes turned wistful, his smile dropping. 'I hope you feel it one day, love. Everyone should at least once. She might be gone but she'll never really be gone, you know? She'll always be there, beside me, smile on her face. It's coming up on twenty-five years, but I ain't never felt no need for anyone else. You know, I still talk to her sometimes. And I know she's listening, even if she don't ever answer back. She's still here, with me.'

Through the windows, the lights of the houses on the other side of the harbour were just visible, flickering out of the reflection of the bar. The breakwater was in darkness, but Rachel thought of William, sitting out there on the end with the water lapping gently against the rocks below his feet, talking to the ghost of his lost father.

'I think she is,' she said, patting Alan on the arm. 'And I think you're lucky.'

Alan smiled. 'I'm the luckiest man in the world,' he said.

24

MOVING FORWARD

How does it feel to have never known how something feels?

Rachel wrote the line, scribbled it out, then wrote it again. Then, beneath, she wrote: *We're all leaves drifting down a river. Some of us run smooth, some of us get caught and struggle. Some of us float on the surface, able to watch the sun, others just beneath, forever caught in the murk of underwater. But we're all heading the same way, and eventually, we'll all get there. But at the end, how does a leaf that's spent its life living in the sun explain the light to one that has never seen it? How can you explain light to something that's known only dark?*

Puffing her cheeks and rolling her eyes, she put her pen down and turned over the sheet of paper.

It was stupid. She'd been on a roll in her notebook, but having failed to find it, she was trying to rediscover the inspiration, but nothing was biting.

"'This is a tale of two fathers,'" she said aloud. "'One who existed and then was gone, another who was never there. Or was he?'"

With a sigh, she stood up. Her shift started in half an

hour, and she was yet to even get dressed. The last couple of days had been constant rain, both inside and out. Linda had gone off for the weekend with Colin, and William had to work, leaving Rachel stuck at home in the flat with nothing to do but stare at the rain and mope about, lamenting her lot in life. She had tried to write, but aside from a few airy-fairy paragraphs about nothing, the inkwell had been dry.

She was just pulling on a sweater when the phone rang. She hurried to pick it up but caught her arm inside the sweater, and by the time she had untangled herself it had rung off. Probably just a wedding venue or an estate agent. Linda could call them back later.

Clara had gone off to visit a museum with a friend, leaving Valerie alone in the shop. When Rachel entered, the old teacher was sitting in a corner, reading a Stephen King novel from the paperbacks rack. She looked up and smiled.

'Ah, I thought you were a customer.'

'Quiet morning?'

'Cathy Ubbers came in for a bag of fudge and some coffees, so in relative terms, not so quiet, but in terms of volume of customers, a bit of a washout.'

'That's too bad. Do you want me to go home?'

Valerie shook her head. 'I like the company. Plus, there's always the chance an out of season bus tour might show up.' She gave a sudden wild grin. 'I wished for it while stirring my cauldron this morning, so we shall see.'

'In the meantime, I'll wipe down the cabinets and reshuffle the postcards.'

Valerie flapped a hand. 'Don't work too hard, and have a coffee for your troubles. This is November after all. There's no reason to be overexerting ourselves, is there?'

The next couple of hours passed in blissful serenity. Cathy Ubbers didn't come back, and Valerie took a nap at a corner table, leaving Rachel to read through a home-life magazine. The rain finally stopped, and a bright November sun lit up Porth Melynos in glittering, dazzling light.

Rachel's shift was almost over, without a customer to be seen, when finally the doorbell tinkled. Valerie was in the kitchen, and Rachel, halfway through an article on restoring faded garden furniture, snapped to attention.

'Hello,' William said with a warm smile. 'I managed to swap out an afternoon shift, and thought I'd surprise you. Do you fancy a walk on the cliffs now the rain has finally stopped?'

'Sure, sounds nice.'

'You might as well just get off now,' Valerie said. 'It doesn't look like that bus tour is going to show up.'

'Okay, thanks.'

They walked down to the harbour. The tide was high, the handful of fishing boats bobbing in the water. A cool wind was whistling down through the valley, but the sky was clear. The cliffs were mottled shades of brown, outlined by couch grass alongside the path as Rachel followed William up a steep slope. Both out of breath, they walked almost in silence until they came to a bench at a lookout point overlooking the harbour. From here the view was the opposite of the one Rachel could see from her grandmother's house; the curve of the harbour directly below, then the village stretching out along the floor of a widening valley. She saw the pub, the café, her mum's apartment building, the library, even the line of the river where she had walked with William. It looked so small, so harmless.

'Coffee?' William asked, pulling a flask out of his bag. 'I got some sandwiches too, if you're hungry.' He shrugged. 'Gorgonzola and pickle if you like a little spice, tuno-mayo if you don't. And if you're half and half, tuna and pickle. I know it's not everyone's cup of tea, but I've always kind of liked it. My dad used to make them.'

'What's this in aid of?' Rachel said. 'I haven't seen you since the weekend.'

'I'm sorry,' William said. 'I had some issues to deal with. Both in and out of work.'

Rachel nodded. In the aftermath of discovering her father's identity, she had sometimes forgotten how she had found William in the first place, fishing without a line off the harbour breakwater. While she had her own problems, he was not a man without his.

'That's okay,' Rachel said, when really it wasn't; she wanted him to talk to her, to let her know how he felt. Sometimes she felt like their relationship was moving forward, other times it felt like it was stuck in quicksand, slowly sinking. *I'm here for you, she wanted to say. Just talk to me.*

William poured the coffee and handed a plastic cup to Rachel. 'I'm sorry,' he said again, and for a moment Rachel feared the worst. He had brought her all the way up here on to the cliffs in order to break up with her. Then, he reached down and pulled something out of his bag.

'I found this in my bag,' he said. 'It must have been in there since we went up to Brentwell last week. I think you must have put it in there by mistake.'

'My notebook … I wondered where it had gone. I couldn't find it anywhere.'

'I didn't notice it before. I'm sorry. I would have brought it straight back if I had.'

Rachel patted his arm. 'Stop saying sorry. It's okay.'

William smiled. 'You know, I'm afraid I didn't know what it was, so I ... opened it ... and I saw what you had started to write about. When I realised, I wanted to close it and put it away, but I ... couldn't. It was so ... compelling.'

Sweat beaded on Rachel's brow despite the cold. 'It was only an idea.'

'"A Tale of Two Fathers." I like it. And your words ... you have a way with them I can only imagine. When I read it, you managed to put into words everything I've wanted to say all these years. It was like ... the way I felt about my father, it was like a fog clouding me. I couldn't make sense of it. Then I read what you'd written, and it made sense. It helped me, Rachel.'

Heat bloomed in her cheeks, and she felt a little tremble at his words. 'So ... you don't think the title is kind of cheesy, and you don't mind me basically intruding on your grief to write about your father?'

William shook his head. 'At first I thought you were just looking for something to make money off, and then I got to know you.'

She could feel him staring at her. She looked up, meeting his eyes. 'And ... what did you think?'

'Whatever I say won't make any difference to who you are,' William said. 'You are you, and I think you're a wonderful person who's had a bit of a run of bad luck. When I look at you, I'm envious.'

Rachel frowned. 'Why?'

'Because you're over it. It's been twenty years since my father disappeared. I know he's gone, and he's never coming back, but what happened haunts me, every day. I've never got over it, and I think, in time, I gave up trying. Everything I've ever done in my life has been as a result of my father's disappearance.' He flapped a hand. 'Look at me. I can't even say it now.'

Quietly, Rachel said, 'Then say it.'

William looked at her. His eyes filled with tears, his bottom lip trembling. 'He's dead,' he whispered, barely loud enough for Rachel to hear. 'My father is dead.'

Rachel grabbed him, pulling him forward before he had a chance to implode, to collapse in on himself like a dying star, to crumple into nothing. She wrapped her arms around him and held him while he cried, staring out at the vast sea, the grey rectangles of ships on the horizon, the white flecks of waves on the swell.

'It'll be all right,' she whispered.

William's sobbing slowly eased. Rachel relaxed her grip on him until he lifted his head to look at her.

'Thank you,' he said.

'I didn't do anything.'

'Yes, you did. You opened me. Like a book. You opened me up and set my feelings free. I've never been able to share how I felt with anyone before. You've helped me more than you could ever know.'

Rachel wasn't sure what to say, so she just offered a smile and nodded. 'You're welcome,' she muttered at last.

'Everything I ever did was out of trying to make sense of it,' William said. 'I've never forgiven myself for that day, and don't think I ever will. My dad shouldn't have died. He was a great, strong, powerful man. He was kind, wise, understanding … and he was taken away from me. I've spent every day of my life regretting that moment. But you … you look forward. You have no regrets. I can't help but envy that.'

'Blame my mother,' Rachel said with a shrug. 'She's at least fifty-percent hippy. And I think it must have embarrassed her a little that my dad was a carpet salesman with a mullet. I was wondering how to tell her that he was killed by a cat, but I think it might be better if I keep that to myself.'

'You have to finish that article,' William said.

'I'm not sure if I can.'

'We're not the only people in the world who've grown up without their fathers,' William said. 'There are others. And if you can put into words some of the feelings we both have, you can help others. You might help yourself, too.'

'How?'

'Because there's a lot more to a story than what you see. Just like there's a lot more to a road than the bit you walk on. There's what lies beneath.'

'You think there's more to my father than a carpet salesman with bad hair who was killed by a cat?'

William nodded. 'Yes,' he said. 'I think there is. But it's more than that. You've already helped me, and I think that you can help yourself by investigating your past a little more. The story isn't over.'

'You don't think so?'

William shook his head. 'Not at all.'

'Well, I hope you're right.' She sighed, turning away from him to look back at the sea. 'I don't know,' she said. 'I'm afraid it'll just turn up more disappointment.'

'You won't know until you try.'

'I'm scared to try.'

'Don't be. If there's anything I've learned from you, it's that I should never be scared of anything.' He squeezed her hand. 'I'll help you. I'll be there if you need me.'

'Really?'

She turned towards him, and the look in his eyes made her stomach give a little lurch.

'Yes,' he said. Then, as a gust of wind rattled them, he leaned forwards, and his lips brushed against hers.

25

BICYCLE RACING

Rachel was sitting on the sofa, a cup of tea beside her and her notebook on her lap, when the door opened and her mum came barging in, a suitcase in one hand and a hold-all around her shoulders.

'How was your trip?'

Linda dropped the suitcase, pulled the hold-all over her head and dumped in on the ground, then kicked the door shut with her heel.

'It had its moments,' she said. 'I enjoyed the buffet lunches.'

'Where did you go, anyway?'

'Museum hopping in Cumbria,' Linda said, the tone of her voice betraying what she thought of such things. 'I mean, I didn't know you could have so many displays of motor-racing vehicles within a five mile radius.'

'Not your thing?'

Linda shrugged. 'Colin liked it.'

'But you'd rather have gone somewhere else?'

'It was what it was,' Linda said.

'The wedding still on?'

Linda flapped her hands. 'I suppose so.'

Rachel grinned. 'Well, if it is, I would like to be a bridesmaid.'

'Really?'

'Mum, don't look so surprised. I'm not saying I'm all that happy about being stepsisters with Cathy, but I've never been a bridesmaid before and I think it could be fun.'

Linda frowned and wandered over. She put one hand on Rachel's shoulder then made a show of peering into each of Rachel's ears.

'Excuse me, is my daughter in there?' she said, making Rachel giggle. 'Where did this sudden positivity come from?'

'It came from you, Mum,' Rachel said. 'I just didn't realise it for a while. You have to live your life, not let it be lived for you. Isn't that right?'

'Well, yes, I suppose so. Always looking forward, never looking back.'

'I was letting things get to me. You know, losing my house, my car, hurting myself, that kind of thing. I thought I was going backwards, but I wasn't.'

'No?'

'In a way, I was still going forwards, but in a roundabout kind of a way.'

Linda lifted an eyebrow. 'Have you been drinking?'

'No! What I mean is that I needed to go back in order to go forward. Do you know what I mean?'

'Kind of like when you're in traffic on a hill and you start pulling away but go backwards before the gear kicks in?'

'Well, I suppose that's one way of looking at it … by the way, Cathy Ubbers just called.'

'Really?'

'Yes. She wanted to know if you were selling Grandma's house. I told her no.'

Linda frowned. 'What? I haven't decided yet. I heard she'd just come into some money, so I suppose she would be a good person to sell it to, having kids and all that—'

'And see her turn it into some kind of Instagram-worthy glass palace?' Rachel shook her head. 'Not a chance.'

'I'm not sure I can afford to have it just sitting there. I'm not made of money, Rachel.'

'You won't have to. I want to live in it.'

'I can't afford—'

'I'll pay rent, Mum. I've checked the local rates online and I'm happy to pay what's fair.' She grinned. 'I mean, I'd expect a bit of a family discount, and since it'll hopefully be mine one day anyway—'

Linda sighed. 'Even if I just charged you enough to cover the rates and the bills, how would you afford it on what you earn?'

'I'll find a way. I've already been into the pub to ask for some shifts, plus I've had a look online to see what else I can do in the meantime. There's some freelance writing work, and—'

'Are you sure? I mean, do you really want to come back here to live?'

Rachel smiled. 'Who can really be sure what's going to happen? All I know right now is that Grandma's house is our family's legacy, and I don't want it sold off to some property developer or some C.E.O. from London who'd only show up for two weeks a year. Even Cathy Ubbers would be a step up from that. I don't want to see our past disappear, Mum. I know you've always taught me to look forward, and rightly so, but the past is the foundation that we stand on, our springboard to the future—'

'Are you sure you didn't swallow a motivational textbook? I can get you some lunch if you're hungry.'

Rachel spread her hands, almost knocking over what remained of her tea. 'I'm already full up on positivity. I get that from you, Mum.'

Linda gave a resigned look, then shrugged. 'Well, I'm glad I was useful for something. I wish that would have filled you up as a teenager. My food bill was astronomical.'

'It was all the badminton, I imagine.'

Linda smiled. 'For the six months you did it. Or was it six weeks?'

Rachel shrugged. 'Something like that. Actually, I was thinking about taking it up again now that I've decided to move back. Got to counteract the extra fudge intake.'

'There's my girl. I might join you. Although I hear young Francis Jenkins is trying to organise a local trail run.'

Rachel grimaced. 'Not sure I could handle that, but maybe next year.'

Linda stared at her a moment, then spread her arms, and came forward to draw Rachel into a warm hug.

'It'll be lovely having my little girl living back in the village,' she said. 'I'm so glad you've decided not to go back to the city.'

'Brentwell's hardly a city, but I take your point,' Rachel said. 'I'll see how it goes. I'm quite excited about it.'

"Quite excited" was only half of it. She felt at least fifty percent terrified, mostly for how she was going to cover the costs of her grandmother's house, having only ever paid rent for a single room. She had no savings, a part time job offering little more than ten hours a week, and no current prospects for more. Geoff, the Horse and Buoy's landlord, had shrugged and said 'Maybe,' whereas her supposed online prospects were a few lowly paid content articles, about which the subject matter she knew very little about.

However, William had inspired her to take a chance. Perhaps, if she imagined it would all work out, then it would.

William.

Wasn't there just a little bit of her who wanted to be closer to him?

He had said he would visit if she decided to go back to Brentwell, but it would add a couple of hours of distance. Here, they were less than thirty minutes apart.

Just thinking about the strange, fishing doctor made all other decision-making cloud over. He was nothing like the guys on the telly, or even the guys from school whom she had once swooned over. He was nothing like Gavin, who was a big, hulking, muscular man, the kind of person who would carry you from a burning building on the palm of one hand. William was slight, almost too thin, no more than an inch or two taller than her, and the kind of man whose face you would never pick out of a crowd. Yet … there was something about him. He was interesting, and kind, and when he smiled, and his eyes really looked at her, she felt something churning inside.

'Earth to Rachel? Don't tell me you're thinking about what colour of carpet you want to put down in Grandma's hall? It's about due for a new one.'

Rachel smiled. 'Actually, I was thinking about leaving them as they are.' *My dad laid those carpets,* she didn't say. Linda probably wouldn't understand. Or maybe, in some deep, carefully hidden and locked-tight vault, she would. But that was a conversation for another day.

～

'What are you sticking those up for?' Valerie asked, frowning as Rachel curled pieces of tape into loops, stuck them to the back of leaf-shapes she had cut out of red and brown card, and pressed them to the front of the display counter.

'It's our autumn season theme,' Rachel said. 'I'm trying to be proactive.'

'It's December next week.'

'So next week we'll put up some Christmas decorations. One season at a time. I think next year we should go full on with it, maybe have a stall outside with some maple branches over the top, perhaps give people a free pine cone.'

'A free pine cone?'

Rachel grinned. 'With a face. Make it out of hazelnuts or bits of felt maybe. Something for the kids.' She lifted a hand and clicked her fingers. 'Perhaps we could do a Saturday workshop? Every participant gets a free bag of fudge at the end. Do we have a website?'

'Not that I'm aware of. I think Clara made a … what's it called? A My Place?'

'Yeah … it might need a little updating. Leave it with me.'

'Do you know how to make a website?'

Rachel shook her head. 'I have no idea. But I can ask someone, or I can figure it out.'

'You are full of buoyancy this morning, aren't you? Are you aware that it's going to rain this afternoon?'

'Good. My new bicycle needs a wash.'

'Bicycle? In Porth Melynos? Are you out of your mind? There's only half a mile of flat road. The rest of this village is so steep I'm surprised they haven't put in steps.'

'I like a challenge. I bought it off Francis Jenkins. He said he's upgraded to some mountain thing.'

'Well, better you than me. I'll stick to my broomstick, thanks.'

Rachel grinned. 'I imagine it's a nightmare with all these coastal winds.'

Valerie winked. 'It takes years of practice to master, dear.' She turned as the doorbell tinkled. 'Oh look, here's Prince Charming. I hope he's got a carriage ready to stop you getting wet on that ridiculous thing. Is it the end of your shift already? I was so enjoying our conversation.'

'You can come around for dinner once I move in,' Rachel said, as William, dressed in a rain jacket over shorts, came over to the counter. 'I'll leave space in the umbrella stand for you to park.'

'You're too kind. So, what are you two idiots up to today?' She gave William a pointed look. 'Aren't you cold?'

He grinned. 'Not yet. I just got off the bus.'

'Are cars that dramatically out of fashion?'

'You have to embrace the modern world, don't you?' Rachel said.

'Look at this,' William said, holding up a piece of creased, rain-spotted paper. 'I was cleaning out the leaflets rack in the waiting room yesterday, and I found this. It's an ad for an uphill cycle race somewhere in Cornwall. I reckon we could train for that.'

Rachel took the piece of paper, smoothed it out a little, and ran her eyes over the details. 'Blue Sands Cove? Mum took me on holiday there once when I was a kid.' She smiled. 'I remember there was a really good fish'n'chips shop. Ah, wait a minute. This race was last summer.'

William nodded. 'I know. But they'll have another one next year, won't they?'

'Probably.'

'So come on, let's go. The one who gives up first buys the ice-creams.'

'You've got about five minutes before it begins to flood,' Valerie said. 'I've been trying to invoke it all morning.'

'See you tomorrow,' Rachel said as she followed William out of the door. Valerie just flapped a hand and gave her a look that said, *rather you than me.*

As soon as they were outside, William turned to Rachel and took her hands in his. Two bicycle helmets bumped against her hip.

'I have a friend who said he'd lend me a van,' he said. 'So that I can help you move.'

'Really?'

William nodded. 'Just give me a few days notice and I'll let him know.'

'I don't think I'll have more than a couple of cases. Mum can probably drive me.'

'If that's what you want, but I'd like to help.'

'If you want to help, I was thinking of changing the wallpaper in the living room. It's a bit peeling in the corners. Me and Mum were on at Grandma for years to change it, but she liked the design.'

'Sure, anything you'd like.'

For a moment they just stared at each other, then in a rush William leaned forward and gave her a quick kiss. Rachel's heart fluttered. As William pulled away, she caught a glimpse of Valerie watching through the fudge shop window. The old teacher smiled and rolled her eyes.

'Here's your helmet,' William said. 'I wasn't sure what colour you liked so I went with gender neutrality and got two brown ones.'

'Ah, thanks. Were they on discount?'

'Half price. The guy wanted me to take all five that were left, but I told him we didn't have kids yet.'

Rachel felt another lurch in her stomach. Six months ago she would have felt dismayed, even terrified at such an aside, but now she just felt a brief moment of elation, as though a rose had bloomed inside her.

'Ah … I imagine they'd want to pick their own colours,' she muttered.

'Shall we?' William said, waving at a corner of the small car park where he had chained his bicycle next to Rachel's. 'By the way, I pumped up your tyres. I think you have a slow puncture.'

'Deliberate sabotage,' Rachel said, digging him in the ribs. 'Because you know I'm going to win.'

'We'll see.'

Overhead, the sky was beginning to cloud over, threatening Valerie's promised rain. There was only one other café still open down by the harbour, where they had shared their first aborted coffee. Rachel still considered it the site of their first unofficial date.

'I've got an idea,' she said, as William clipped his helmet on. 'It looks like it's going to rain, so why don't we just go down to the harbour, drink coffee and eat pasties, and discuss tactics?'

William looked at her, a small smile spreading across his lips. 'I think that's a great idea,' he said. 'Plus, it would probably be good to fuel up first, wouldn't it?'

26

LOTTERY

Rachel lifted the envelope and gave it a quick kiss before putting it into the postbox. 'Good luck,' she whispered as she listened to the dull thud of it landing on top of the rest of the post waiting for collection. It was a ceremonial thing; she had also emailed a copy, but this was like something she needed to do to really feel like a journalist: her first mailed submission. She fully expected to receive a rejection either by return of post or online within hours, or perhaps not even at all, but there was still that inkling of hope remaining, a tiny sliver of a dream that perhaps every writer experienced. Giving the corner of the postbox a pat, she took a deep breath and headed for home.

Linda was washing up the lunch plates in the kitchen. As Rachel came in, she felt a brief pang of guilt that she hadn't told her mother about the article. Perhaps, if it was accepted, she would.

'I have good news,' Linda said, setting the last plate down in the rack and grabbing a towel off a rail. 'Colin and me … we're back on.'

'Really? Mum, that's great. If that's what you want. When's the big day?'

'Well, we've decided to not to rush into things. We're thinking about doing it next summer.' She grinned. 'It gives me plenty of time to back out if necessary. Do you remember that place in Cornwall we went to when you were a kid? Blue Sands? We were thinking of doing it there. Beach wedding and all.'

'Blue Sands Cove? What made you choose there?'

Linda nodded at the dining room table. 'You left some leaflet lying around, and it got me thinking. Wouldn't that be nice? It was a delightful little place. Perhaps we could do it on the same weekend of that race. Were you actually planning to do it? I saw the bike. Nothing slips past me, love.'

'It seems not … well, I suppose I'll have to, won't I?'

Linda clapped her hands together loud enough to make Rachel jump. 'Fantastic. I do love to be an inspiration. It would give both of us the motivation to not back out. And you never know, if you and William stay together, we could even have a double wedding.'

Rachel felt her cheeks pluming like the robin's breasts on the Christmas cards she'd seen stocked in local shops as thoughts turned to the next major event on the calendar.

'I don't think we're quite ready for that,' she muttered.

'Well, who knows what might be around the corner,' she said. 'By the way, someone called, asking to speak to you. Someone called Todd.'

'Todd?'

'You look surprised. Is he some old boyfriend from Brentwell?'

'Ah, no, nothing like that.'

'Well, he asked you to call him. He said you should

have his number, but if not, he left it. I wrote it down on the pad over there.'

'Thanks.'

Rachel waited until Linda had headed out to work before calling Todd back. Her hands were shaking as she held the phone against her ear. What did he want? Surely it wasn't just a social call? Was she about to find out that she was wrong, that the man she thought was her dad wasn't actually him? She thought about the article she had just posted off to the BBC website. Would she need to rewrite it, or just throw the whole thing in the bin?

'Hello, Evans' Carpets.'

'Ah ... Todd? It's Rachel.'

'Rachel? Aha, thanks for calling. Ah, you're wondering, aren't you? Why I called?' A chuckle, his nervousness showing through. 'I have something I'd like to talk to you about. Any chance you can pop up? It'll be easier in person.'

'To Brentwell?'

'Yeah, if possible. I mean, we could meet on Dartmoor if you like, but it's a bit gloomy at this time of year, and the wind ... well, yeah.'

Rachel nodded. 'Sure.'

∼

Todd suggested a little café down the street from Evans' Carpets, just to 'get out for a while.' Rachel had come alone; William had offered, but she sensed from Todd's voice that this was something she had to do by herself. Now, she watched as Todd pulled a plastic file out of his bag and set it down on the table.

'Had a chat to Dad,' he said. 'Took a while to get around to it, you know? Sorry. He told me some stuff I didn't know, and I thought you'd want to be in on the loop.'

He opened the file and withdrew a smaller clear plastic envelope. Inside was a small picture of a child, dressed in dungarees and wearing a sun hat, standing beside a hydrangea adorned with vibrant purple flowers. Rachel gasped.

'Where did you get this?'

'That's you, isn't it?' Todd said.

'Yes. My mother has the same picture, or at least a really similar one. I was about three. That's my grandmother's garden. Where did you get it?'

'It was found in Uncle's wallet when he died. Dad kept it, put it away with the rest of Uncle's things.'

'And he didn't try to find me?'

Todd looked pained. 'Yeah … I dunno. I think he might have asked around, but Uncle was a bit of a free wheeler, you know what I mean? I think Dad was worried about opening too many cans of worms. But anyway, there's the other thing.'

'What other thing?'

Todd reached back into the file and pulled out a wad of A4 paper. It looked like a contract of some kind, all fine print, graphs and tables of figures.

'You were named in Uncle's will.'

'What?'

Todd turned over a page and read, '"The girl in the photograph is my daughter. Twenty-five percent of my share of Evans' Carpets profits should be saved in a trust for when she comes." That make any sense to you? Dad was a man of his word. But he set it all up years ago and promptly forgot about it. In any case, after I mentioned you showing up, he pulled out the docs, and here they are.' Todd grinned like a happy dog wanting a pat on the head.

'Of course, you'll need to be formally identified, but that shouldn't be difficult. Welcome to the family.'

'I still don't … are you saying … I don't really know what you're saying.'

'For the last twenty odd years Evans' Carpets has been paying twenty-five percent of Uncle's share of the profits into a trust fund that will soon belong to you.' Todd rifled through the pages and pulled out a sheet of paper. 'Obviously it's still ongoing, but with current interest rates and all that, the current total is about this.'

He pointed to a number on the page, and Rachel's jaw almost hit the table.

'Oh my god. That's nearly three hundred thousand pounds.'

'You came here by bus, right? Probably about now you could afford a car. I know a guy who'd do you a great deal on an almost-new if you're interested—'

Rachel began to filter Todd out. Her whole estimation of her father had suddenly shifted. He had not only known her, but he had loved her, and he had provided for her too. The caricature of a man who had been scared to death by a cat had been completely redrawn.

'Are you all right? I mean, this is a bit of a champagne moment, isn't it?'

With tears in her eyes, Rachel said, 'I wrote something. Now I have to write it again.'

~

She supposed every writer had been through it. Finding the typo after the submission was sent, addressing her cover letter accidentally to a Mrs. instead of a Ms., getting a letter in her postcode wrong. With an email explaining she had written the whole thing over, followed by a posted envelope explaining the same thing, Rachel wondered if she would be blacklisted by the BBC website's submissions department forever, or perhaps be the subject of some departmental joke, or maybe even just ignored. Perhaps that was better.

To make herself feel better, she went for an afternoon pint in the Horse and Buoy. The only other customer was Alan Marsh, sipping quietly on a pint as he leaned over the bar.

'Hello again, lass. About time Geoff got a stool with your name on it. What's the occasion?'

'I'm going through a few strange days,' Rachel said.

'Ah, season's turn, always has that effect,' Alan said. 'Got your tree out yet? My old Maggie always said no earlier than December tenth. What with shops these days, you'd think the season kicked off soon as the pumpkins got put away.'

'It's certainly been an autumn I'll never forget,' Rachel said.

'Aye, nice to have one that 'tis memorable,' Alan said. 'When you get to my age, they tend to blend into one. I hear on the grapevine that you're moving into your old grandmother's place.'

Rachel lifted an eyebrow, surprised how quickly news could travel. 'That's right,' she said. 'I couldn't bear to let it leave the family, and since Mum didn't want to live there, I didn't have a lot of choice.'

'Ain't gonna find a better view,' Alan said. 'Garden's gonna need a bit of work come spring. You might be able to tempt me out of retirement for a cup of tea and a biscuit once in a while.'

Rachel smiled. 'Thanks, Alan.'

'No one cuts a hedge in Porth Melynos like me. Dying art, that is.'

'I won't forget.'

'That mother of yours still getting married?'

Rachel laughed. 'As far as I know. She's off and on about it.'

'Well, better late than never. I'll believe it when I see it, though. Not one to be nailed down, is our Linda. I mean, she's always been a free spirit. I remember once when it looked like it might happen, but never did.'

Rachel turned in her stool. 'Alan, what do you mean?'

The old man looked confused, as though the words had come out unheeded. 'Ah, my old mind's not what it was. And you know, I've had a pint….'

'Was my mother married before?'

'No, no. But there was this time I was up your grandmother's, and I overheard something … I don't remember too well now.'

'What?'

Alan shifted. 'I think you'd better ask her about that. Your mother, I mean. I don't know that your grandmother is up to too much conversation these days.' He chuckled, then excused himself and shuffled off in the direction of the toilet.

Rachel stared at her pint, barely touched. Then, making up her mind, she got down off her stool, pushed her pint across towards Alan's seat, and headed for the door.

It was time to get some answers.

27

UNDER THE SURFACE

Linda was washing up in the kitchen. Rachel took the key off the hook, locked the door on the inside, and then went over to the window. She didn't want to lose the key completely, so she pulled open the window, leaned out, and dropped it carefully into the bushes below.

If that was what it took to get some information out of her mother, then so be it.

'Mum? Can I have a word?'

Linda looked up. 'Sure. Tea?'

'Thanks.'

Linda made two cups of tea and carried them over to the coffee table. Rachel sat down on an armchair, facing her mother on the sofa.

'Is this about Grandma's house?' Linda asked. 'If you think it's too much, you can change your mind. I can still put it on the market. Or has something happened with William? I know he seemed nice, but you just don't know with some people—'

'Mum, I found Dad.'

Linda's mouth snapped shut. She looked down at the

table, frowning, then pulled up her sleeve and looked at her watch.

'Oh, I really should get on. I wanted to nip to the shops for some bread before my shift starts—'

'I just thought you'd like to know.'

Linda appeared to be ignoring her. Her hands flapped around, moving magazines back and forth, then she got up and headed for the door.

'Sorry, but we're having this conversation,' Rachel said, as Linda's hand closed over the door handle. 'I've waited long enough.'

Linda rattled the door, then reached for the key hook. As she lifted a tattered cluster of old souvenirs and a ragged grey bunny Rachel had got her from the Peter Rabbit Museum in the Lake District, she let out a long sigh.

'Mum, please.'

Linda gave the door another weak shake, more optimistic than anything, then turned. Head lowered, she returned to the sofa and sat down like a schoolgirl about to be scolded over a poor report.

'Mum, look at me.'

Linda slowly lifted her head.

'Mum, can I just say something? You're not just my mum, you know. You're also my best friend. You've done everything for me. Given me everything I've ever asked for, lifted me up when I was down, leveled me out when I was getting too big for myself. You're the perfect mother, and I couldn't have asked for a better one.'

'Oh, Rachel. I think I'm going to cry.'

Rachel already had tears in her eyes, but she was on a roll, and there were things she needed to say that she might never get a chance to say again. She took a deep breath.

'I never wondered about Dad because I never needed

to. You were all the parent I needed. I never wanted for anything, and I always felt so loved. Thank you, Mum.'

Linda was crying now, too. Rachel wanted to hug her, but she was afraid of being derailed, of losing her best chance to discover the truth.

'Rachel, I only ever wanted what was best for you.'

'And you got it right, Mum. You got everything right. I might have been going through a bit of a blip, but I'm over that now. I've kind of got myself sorted out. However, I'm twenty-three years old. And there are some things that I need to know. Nothing will change between us. Nothing. Call it curiosity, if you like, but I need to know about Dad. I need to know what kind of person he was.'

Linda looked up. 'Was? Then you know.'

Rachel nodded. 'And clearly so do you. Tell me, Mum.'

Linda stood up, and for a moment Rachel thought she meant to do something crazy, like shoulder-barge her way through the front door, or attempt to squeeze through the narrow gap left by the open window and jump for the ground below. Then Linda said, 'Just wait a moment. There's something I should show you. I suppose there won't be a better time.'

She went into her bedroom. Rachel stared after her, feeling blood pumping in her temples. Through the open window, a cool breeze drifted in, making her shiver. She was just thinking about getting up and closing it when Linda reappeared, carrying a tiny box cupped in both hands.

'People in this town have always judged me,' Linda said, sitting back down. She stared at the box in her hands, a tiny, felt-covered square. 'I've always been free-spirited Linda, and I'm okay with that. But what you see is not always everything.'

Rachel smiled. William, Cathy, even Valerie and

Francis, even Alan Marsh … was there anyone she had met since her return who hadn't revealed another side to their personalities? Was there anyone she had met who had been the person they had seemed at first glance?

Linda opened the little box to reveal a beautiful ring. A single diamond sparkled, making Rachel gasp.

'I've kept it all these years,' Linda said.

'Mum, I—'

'I did what I had to do to bring you up right,' Linda said. 'I didn't want you to grow up always looking over your shoulder. I wanted you to look forward, to be positive. Sometimes things happen that we can't change, but we can't let them be chains around our necks.'

'He asked you to marry him?'

Linda smiled, tears in her eyes. 'The night he died. It wasn't going to work, I knew it wasn't. It was only a fling, but he wanted to be a father to you. He was always coming down to see you, and Grandma played the game too. You have no idea how many times she changed those carpets.'

Linda gave a damp chuckle, and Rachel couldn't help but smile. 'He was the strangest of men on the outside,' Linda continued. 'His hair … oh god, his hair. It was like someone had glued a shaggy dog to his head. I look back now and I don't know what I was thinking … but he was one of those people who was just kind of … interesting. Like a surprise package. I was drawn in, completely taken with him.' She sighed. 'But it didn't last. I wasn't that sort of person. After you were born, though, and I told him, he just changed. He wanted to be your father, and not just showing up once every couple of months, he wanted to be there for you. He didn't ask me to marry him for me, he asked me for you.'

Rachel's hands were shaking. She picked up her tea, only for a tear to plop into the water, breaking the film that had formed across the surface. Rachel wiped the gunk away with a finger, then took a sip, grimacing to find that the tea had already gone cold.

'What did you say?' she asked.

'I said … I'd think about it. We weren't in love with each other, and we both knew it. But he was a good man. And we both wanted what was best for you, so I was prepared to do that. To think about it.' Linda sighed. 'And then I heard what had happened. Actually, I read it in the newspaper the next day. And it was like….' She shook her head. 'Like my decision was made for me. It made me focus. It made me focus on you. And from that day onwards, I did everything I could to make you happy. I never wanted you to look back, to wonder what might have been.'

'Mum, I don't know what to say.'

'Things are what they are,' Linda said. 'But … I'm glad you found him in the end. I mean that. I don't suppose it matters now, but he was a good man, and I think he would have been a good father.'

'I know he would have,' Rachel said. 'But that doesn't change anything between us. You were the best mother, Mum. You still are.'

This time, Rachel got up, leaned over the coffee table and pulled Linda forward into a hug.

'Are you sure things are okay between us?' Linda asked against Rachel's shoulder.

'Yes, Mum, they are.'

'I'm glad. But look, I really have to get to work. You can unlock the door now.'

Rachel pulled away. 'I'm afraid I threw the keys out of the window.'

'What about your key?'

'Yeah … I left it at work yesterday.'

'Then how are we supposed to get out of the flat? It's too high to jump. I'm as brittle as a dry cracker and I doubt your bad foot would appreciate it.'

Rachel grinned. 'Can't you just call Colin? After all, he was a fireman, wasn't he?'

28

HOUSEWARMING

'Where do you want this one?' William said, carrying a box of clothes into the hall.

'Just put it over there,' Rachel said, puffing out her chest with pride, feeling like a bird staking out its territory. 'I'll deal with it later. I think it's time for coffee, don't you?'

William smiled. 'Good idea.' As he followed Rachel into the kitchen, he added, 'You know, we should go out somewhere for dinner, to celebrate.'

She turned and met his eyes. He gazed at her gently, a smile on his face, and she knew that everything would be all right. She waited while he came over, took her hands in his, and gave her a light kiss.

'That sounds nice,' she said. 'It'll have to be outside the village. I think everything nearby is closed now, except for the pub.'

'We'll think of somewhere.'

Rachel nodded. 'I'd also like to have a housewarming party.'

'Really?'

'Yes. Once I'm settled in. Although I might have to

double down with Christmas. By the time I'm unpacked, it'll be about time to start putting up decorations, so perhaps I'll make it a Christmas party at the same time.'

'I think your dad would be proud of you,' William said.

'Why?'

'I can't claim that I know much about him, but you've definitely got a bit of his entrepreneurial spirit. That never-give-up attitude.'

'Oh, I gave up. I gave up plenty of times. It was you who helped me through it.'

'I didn't do anything. Maybe offered a little advice. But isn't that what boyfriends are for?'

Boyfriend. It sounded nice. Perhaps one day it might be something more, but for now Rachel was content.

'And for rubbing toes,' she said.

'Got it.'

'You know, your dad would be proud of you too. More than you can imagine.'

William nodded. 'I hope so.'

He was about to say something more when the doorbell buzzed.

'I'm not expecting anyone,' Rachel said, reluctantly letting go of his hands to go and answer it.

To her surprise, Gary, the local postman, stood on the step, a box in his arms, a smaller letter balanced on top.

'Hi Rachel,' he said. 'Your mum said you'd moved. Can you grab that letter, then sign for this box?'

'No problem. Thanks, Gary.'

'Have a nice day.'

As Gary turned and whistled as he headed back to his van, Rachel carried the box back into the living room. William was busying himself with making coffee, but now looked up and frowned.

'Getting post already?'

'Seems like it. I wonder ... oh.'

'What is it?'

She held up the letter to reveal a familiar logo. 'Oh my. Or as Cathy might say, O.M.G. It's probably a rejection, but you never know.'

'Only one way to find out.'

Rachel grimaced and held out the envelope to William. 'Can you open it for me? I'm scared.'

William shook his head. 'Absolutely not. This is your destiny. Go and get it.'

Rachel stared at the envelope. The article hadn't been that great. It would likely be a form letter, a standard rejection. Still, it would get the ball rolling, and there were other magazines that might be interested. Plus, it was her first article, and she was hardly a seasoned pro—

She ran a finger inside the seal, tearing a line across the top. With shaking fingers, she pulled out the folded sheet of paper inside. At first, she was so nervous she wasn't even sure she could read it, as though it had been written in a foreign language just to fool with her. Then—

'"*Dear Ms. Castle, thank you for your submission. I would like to say ...*" No way! They took it! Ahhh!'

'You sound like you're in pain. Luckily I'm a doctor.'

It took Rachel a few more seconds of bouncing around the room to calm down. William came over and gave her a warm hug.

'February 10th,' she said, reading over his shoulder. 'The editor says here she wants pictures. Oh my god. And have I written or considered writing anything else?'

'Fantastic,' William said. 'I knew you could do it.'

Rachel's smile dropped. 'I feel like a fraud. I've exploited you and my mother, and my father's family.'

William shook his head. 'You've done nothing of the sort. I've read it. It made me cry, but in a good way. You somehow managed to put into words all the feelings I've been unable to come to terms with. I feel like finally I can move on with my life, and that's thanks to you. And I won't be the only one. Your article will help people, Rachel.'

'I hope so. But you know … I'm still worried about it.'

'Of course. That's natural. But it'll get easier.'

The other box was still sitting on the dining room table. 'I wonder what's in there?'

William smiled. 'Only one way to find out.'

He passed her a knife from a drawer and she gently cut the tape sealing the box. She lifted the flaps and let out a little gasp of surprise.

On the top sat a piece of A4 paper with a crude child's drawing of a house and a stick man standing outside.

'I think that's supposed to be you,' William said.

Underneath, someone clearly a little more literate had written, *Happy housewarming, love Cathy, Gav, and family xxx.*

'Looks like you'll have to have that party,' William said. 'What did she send you?'

Rachel lifted the sheet of paper, then let out a little laugh. 'Six bottles of peach schnapps,' she said. 'I'm going to have to invite her, aren't I? There's no way I can drink all this.'

'Well, there's probably a more than fifty percent chance you're going to be stepsisters,' William said. 'Has your mum decided yet?'

'No … but she said she was leaning more towards yes than to no. I think rescuing us from the house without having to break down the front door definitely angled the needle towards yes a little. Particularly after Colin showed up in full fireman uniform.'

'Welcome to the beginning of your new life,' William said, pulling her close again. 'How do you like it?'

Rachel looked up at him. 'It definitely has its perks,' she said. 'Have you made that coffee yet?'

'Nearly.'

'Good. Because after that there's my toes to deal with, and then there's a table I need moved, and after that you can take me out for dinner. How's that for a plan?'

'William smiled. 'Perfect,' he said.

∼

Acknowledgements

Many thanks goes to Elizabeth Mackey for the cover, Jenny Avery for your endless wisdom, Paige for the editorial stuff, and also to my eternal muses Jenny Twist and John Daulton, whose words of encouragement got me where I am today, nearly ten years after the journey started.

Lastly, but certainly not least, many thanks goes to my wonderful Patreon supporters:

Carl Rod, Rosemary Kenny, Jane Ornelas, Ron, Betty Martin, Gail Beth Le Vine, Anja Peerdeman, Sharon Kenneson, Jennie Brown, Leigh McEwan, Amaranth Dawe, Janet Hodgson, and Katherine Crispin

and to everyone's who's bought me a coffee recently:

Sheri, Niall, Amelie, Paul, Laurie, Aileen, Att, Irena, Michael, and Lindsay

You guys are fantastic and your support means so much.

For more information:
www.amillionmilesfromanywhere.net

Printed in Great Britain
by Amazon